THE

SORCERER'S
CONCUBINE

THE TELEPATH AND THE SORCERER BOOK ONE

Jaclyn Dolamore

To Heather, for always knowing when I need a phone call from a friend

CHAPTER ONE

Most of the men who came to the House of Perfumed
Ribbons knew what they wanted. The girls came in a few classic
types. There were the innocents with their youthful air. The
vixens, sultry and experienced—the only girls who had been with
men before. The bodyguards, trained in fighting. The "Little
Wives" who would provide domestic comforts along with the
physical, and the entertainer girls who could play an instrument
and make witty conversation.

Velsa already knew she was not a bodyguard or a little wife,
or she would have been pulled aside at a younger age to learn
how to cook and nurse, or wield a bow and arrow. And certainly
she was not a vixen, who periodically spent time with a more
experienced male concubine.

She had spent hours upon hours plucking the strings of a
bastir, in the hopes of being an entertainer. She figured any man
who came to buy an entertainer girl must be well educated and
appreciate the arts; maybe he would value her mind and not just
her body.

Now that Velsa was finally old enough to be acquired, she
found out exactly where she stood.

"You'll be with the Village Girls," said Dalarsha, the House
Mother.

"The Village Girls?" Velsa was dismayed. "But…"

"I know, you have been very diligent with your music

practice, but I'm afraid you just haven't achieved the level of skill men will expect. You still make mistakes. There's nothing wrong with being a Village Girl."

"There's nothing interesting about being a Village Girl either," Velsa said.

"Listen, my dear," Dalarsha said. "You don't need to be interesting. Men don't really care about that anyway. Just give them your sweetest face, and some man will be happy to treat you well."

Soon Velsa would be a stranger's possession. With luck, he would be kind. He would treasure her and give her gifts and take her to parties dressed in fine clothes to show off his wealth. But every girl knew they might not have that sort of luck.

And even the luckiest girls had still been created for a single purpose, in the end. Even a man who was generous and complimented her beauty would expect to have his way with her, any time it pleased him.

"Anyway," Dalarsha said, more solemnly. "You have a golden band. We don't want you to seem too dangerous."

Velsa put a hand to the circle of gold locked around her throat. The enchanted band suppressed the telepathic abilities she had been born with. Without that assurance, no man would buy her—they wouldn't feel safe. But even so, many Daramon men didn't trust telepaths, and they wouldn't look twice at a girl with her powers.

The girls who had come of age before her were excited to welcome her into the front of the House. They all couldn't help but look forward to this rite of passage, even as they feared it, because either way, it meant they were grown women, and the course of their lives would soon be determined. It was a tradition, on that first night, for all the girls to lend the new initiate their favorite pieces of clothing, clothes the girls often scrounged their tips to buy in the hopes of attracting the finest and wealthiest of men.

If the girl was lucky enough to be chosen on her very first

2

night, all the beautiful clothes would go with her. It was a game that someone won every year or so. When this happened, word quickly leaked back to the younger girls who had not yet seen the front of the House, and they would all lament the necklaces and headdresses and shoes that would never be seen again, most of them purchased with the tips they earned with their charms.

"If I lose my best stockings, I can always buy more. It's too much fun to dress you up like a princess," said Pia, one of the vixen girls. "And it helps with the nerves."

"Hopefully," Velsa said. Her voice was a little shaky. She was standing in her chemise in front of the mirror, nearly as naked as she'd ever been, unused to being the center of attention.

"First, my dragon stockings!" Pia exclaimed, waving her hand to flirtatious little Bari, who presented the neatly folded stockings like a crown. Velsa remembered Pia from their school days, before Pia came of age and went into the house a few months ago. She seemed more jovial than Velsa remembered, as if she actually preferred male attention to education.

Velsa pulled each silk stocking onto her legs slowly, admiring the way the design unfolded. The tails of the dragons started at her feet, the sinuous golden bodies running all the way up above her knees. A tiny button had been sewn onto the back of Velsa's legs, to help keep the stockings up, and over these Pia tied yellow satin ribbons snug around Velsa's thighs. Her bows were so perfect that Velsa would have to ask her how to do them later.

"Lift your arms," Pia said.

"You don't have to dress me."

"We must dress you! Just for today. Princess Velsa. No, *Queen* Velsa. Why settle?" Pia slid an under-robe over her shoulders. This was a simple garment, but over it came a beautiful dark red sash of fabric woven and dyed in Halnari, where some of the finest textiles were made—especially sashes, which the Halnari women also favored. Even as Pia was tying the sash at the back of Velsa's narrow waist, Amleisa was stuffing her feet into heeled shoes made of red brocade.

3

"Is—is there anything I should know?" Velsa asked, fighting off another wave of panic. "When the men come in?"

"Not really," Bari said. "Just bow and look shy and ask them a few questions about their lives and then look impressed—the men will love you."

"Don't smell the men," Pia said breezily.

The other girls laughed, but Velsa's innards shifted with fear. "Are flesh and blood men really that bad?"

"Sometimes," Pia said. "Depends on where they're from. The city merchants are the worst. Like they have no time to bathe and living on top of one another has dulled their sense of smell."

"The girls we really should be asking for advice are the ones who have already left," Amleisa said, with a wistful air.

When girls were chosen, occasionally they still wrote letters back to the House, but usually they were never heard from again. Dalarsha told them that men didn't like to consider the previous lives of the girls they purchased. They wanted to believe they were buying a newly minted person, who had been created just for them, not so much a frightened and inexperienced girl, as a toy fresh out of the box, created to be played with. Not that Velsa's teachers worded it like that exactly, but she understood the unspoken truth.

It didn't seem fair or reasonable to Velsa, that she should pretend the last eighteen years of her life had never existed. Even Fanarlem girls had to grow up on the inside, no matter how their bodies looked on the outside.

Still, Velsa knew she was fortunate to have been created for the House of Perfumed Ribbons. It was renowned across the region as the most reputable place to purchase a Fanarlem concubine, because the girls were well cared for and allowed to come of age in a natural way. In fact, the older girls said some men didn't like to buy from their House because the girls seemed a little *too* real. The men almost felt like they were buying flesh and blood girls, and *that* was entirely illegal and immoral.

But what Fanarlem girl didn't want to be seen as a flesh and blood girl?

4

Pia had pinned up the corners of Velsa's under-robe so her stockings could be seen in full. Velsa felt exposed, but of course that was the idea. And the next garment was an over-robe, which she could pull around her body to hide if she felt the need, although this was certainly not advised if she wanted to be acquired…unless, of course, the man liked his girl to be demure. But that was usually the province of the innocents. This over-robe was made of expensive dark red silk and had a dramatic collar that fanned over her shoulders, made of black brocade edged in silver thread.

The final touch were two clips in her hair, just above her ears, in the fashionable shape of wings.

Bari sprayed a mist of floral perfume around Velsa's neck. Velsa sniffed the delicate floral fragrance. It made her think of spring, even on a rainy autumn night.

"That's how Village Girls smell," Pia teased, like it was a bad thing. Vixens didn't smell of spring flowers, but of spice and musk.

"Now what?" Velsa asked.

"Now, we wait," Bari said.

Night was creeping in, and the district was springing to life. Dalarsha placed lit lanterns in the windows. The girls were grouped into different rooms according to their general type, so Dalarsha could steer the visitors toward girls of interest and keep them separate as much as possible, so the girls in each room could shower all their attention on one or two men at a time. Each room was decorated to reflect the girls inside, so the Little Wives gathered around a hearth making popcorn or roasted nuts while the men settled into cushy chairs, and the vixens had a pleasure den of wispy curtains and pillows on the floor. The Village Girls had a parlor with a sofa and a crackling fireplace, and walls decorated with romantic prints of beautiful girls looking over their shoulders, as if they were all beckoning the men to follow.

Every night, many men came simply out of curiosity, to see

the famous Fanarlem concubines. In all the world, most Fanarlem were created as slaves, particularly for working in mines or with dangerous chemicals and dyes: all the jobs that were hazardous to flesh and blood people. Many households also kept a Fanarlem slave to do the most grueling household labor.

It cost far more to make a Fanarlem like Velsa. *Fanar lem*—it meant, literally, a person made from scraps. An animated rag doll. Velsa was certainly not made from scraps. Her innards were carefully constructed to mimic the muscles of a living woman, and her skin was made from soft yet durable fabrics. Her hair was real and thick, and her face had been shaped by a master craftsman. Spells were woven through every aspect of her body, to make it look and feel even more real.

Still, she had been reminded all her life that she was still a lesser being, a cursed soul. As soon as the girls learned to read, they were handed moral tales of noble Fanarlem suffering. The girls even learned penmanship by copying phrases like, "My soul is redeemed by following the orders of my masters" and "It is my greatest joy and virtue to surrender my will and accept my place in the world."

She must have done some misdeed in her past life, or else her soul would have been too strong to have been called into an artificial body. If her future master was kind to her, she should count herself lucky. If he was not, she should also count herself lucky, because his cruelty would be her penance, and her reward would come in the next life.

Velsa knew it was true.

But the words never failed to taste bitter.

She waited in the softly lit room with Amleisa and Nraya, the other Village Girls. Just outside the window, a few men came down the street, pointing up at the sign for the House of Perfumed Ribbons. It depicted a hand with stitches at the wrist, with a ribbon tied around one of its fingers.

"*Skarnwen!*" jeered one of the prostitutes who were all over the streets in this district. Tonight a few of them were hiding out under the balcony of the house across the way, keeping out of the rain.

Skarnwen was slang for men who liked dolls more than real women. But plenty of men liked both. The men ignored them and moved to the door, disappearing from Velsa's view.

Now she heard the door open. A few male voices entered. The House of Perfumed Ribbons was an attraction on the streets of Nisa. Most of the men had no intent to buy, but they paid a few coins just to get in the door and often they also tipped the girls. When Dalarsha pointed a man their way, Amleisa and Nraya rushed to greet him. Velsa was just a step behind.

"Welcome, sir," they chorused.

Amleisa brushed a few raindrops off his cloak. "It's a little wet out tonight, isn't it?"

The man chuckled nervously. "Yes, it is." He stared at them like they were curiosities rather than beautiful women.

"You must be nice to Velsa," Amleisa said. "It's her first day here."

"Oh is that so?" He looked at Velsa now. "Don't be shy."

She bowed as she had been taught, pointing one toe forward, sweeping one arm out. "No, sir."

Nraya nudged her. "Maybe you should offer this lovely man a drink." She flashed the man a brief smile.

Lovely man? Hardly. He was reasonably handsome, like most Daramon men. If they could afford it, they would go to a Halnari shapeshifter and have any unattractive features smoothed into beauty. Their age was hard to determine because they wouldn't allow many wrinkles to show. But you couldn't shape-shift the look in a man's eyes, and in his she saw a vague excitement paired with something calculating.

Velsa crossed the room, past the luxurious sofa upholstered in gold fabric that glowed in the lamp-light, to a table covered in bottles. He watched her every move. She poured a glass of diluted wine. Her hands were still a little shaky but no one seemed to notice. "Sir." She offered the glass.

He drank, beginning to warm to their presence. He let Amleisa take his arm and lead him to the sofa. Once he was

7

sitting, she slowly drew away, her expression coy. He grabbed her arm and pulled her body down, so she tumbled onto his lap.

"You're such a little thing," he murmured.

"You can handle two of us, then," Amleisa said. Like all the girls, Amleisa was just a little older than Velsa; they had grown up together, until Amleisa turned eighteen and moved to the front of the House. It was so odd to see her flirting like this, playing the part so well.

Amleisa was looking at Velsa, a wordless beckon. Velsa was frozen.

"Don't be shy," the man repeated. "I won't hurt you."

Velsa didn't want Dalarsha to hear that she had stuck herself in a corner all night.

I was made for this. I have no choice.

She forced herself to sit on the man's other knee. He slid his hand up her back. His skin was warm. His face was rough with stubble and his clothes were dusty from travel. Velsa reminded herself not to sniff, in case he was one of the smelly ones Pia warned her about. Fanarlem didn't have to breathe, so smelling was always a conscious act, but even without a scent to accompany his rugged body, the solid feel of his thigh beneath her was disconcerting. He seemed so much stronger and earthier than her.

His hand worked its way beneath the edge of her over-robe, and now it touched the sash at her waist. "Don't be scared."

She could no longer look at him. She looked at Amleisa's hand instead.

He isn't allowed to do anything to me unless he buys me. If he touched her beneath her clothes, she could scream and Dalarsha would come and tell him he must pay.

But if he had the money, he could do anything he liked to her. He could take her home with him. He could trap her inside his house, away from anyone she might call a friend. This scared her more than anything; the prospect of being trapped.

Fear threatened to rip a scream from her throat. If she let

8

out a single cry, if she sprung off the man's lap, all the other girls would tease her. They all went through this, didn't they? And surely none of them enjoyed it, but they pretended so well.

So many of the girls who were bought were never heard from again. The world beyond this house was largely a mystery and no one would save her from its horrors. She had to accept this.

This was a fact she had been told all her life, and yet it was as if she had just heard it for the first time. As if she had denied the reality of it until this very moment, when the reality had a large hand spread across her back.

"Darling…" Amleisa smoothed Velsa's hair. "It's all right. He's a nice gentleman. Aren't you?"

"Of course I am," he said. "I think you're both beautiful."

Nraya sat down beside them. "Where are you from?" she asked.

"Baltia."

"Oh, what a long journey! I bet you've never seen a Fanarlem girl like us before."

"Certainly not like you. Never like you." His hand rested on Velsa's hip now and he squeezed her skin. She stiffened with a gasp, but he didn't even react.

"Just like a real girl," he said approvingly.

She had never felt so alone—so exposed. No one cared that she was terrified. And this was only the beginning…

As he finished his drink, Nraya smoothly nudged Velsa out of the way and took her place on the man's knee, giving Velsa time to collect herself.

Before long, he was moving on, curious about the other girls in the House. Amleisa and Nraya rushed to reassure Velsa. "You did just fine," Amleisa said. "The first one is always the worst."

"Well—" Nraya interjected. "Except occasionally they are really awful. He wasn't so bad."

Amleisa gave her a sharp look. "Let's not mention that today."

9

"I already *know*," Velsa said. "I've heard all the stories. I just never understood how it would really feel... How can you stand it, knowing that the worst of men could own you at any moment? Any moment, he might walk in the door and your life would be over?"

"Shh." Amleisa was smoothing her hair again. "You know what they say. Even the worst of it will wash our sins away."

No one bought Velsa that day. A tiny piece of her was disappointed, to take off the embroidered stockings and the fine robes. Tomorrow she would wear her own new concubines robes; still expensive, but not as expensive as the ones tips could buy. It was a point of pride to be one of the rare few who was chosen on the first day, and shameful to linger in the House for months, passed over again and again. One girl had remained in the House for three years, such an embarrassingly long time that men who came to visit more than once began commenting on her continuing existence there. On her twenty-first birthday, she finally left and went to the Fanarlem brothel in Porstan.

Nraya was right. The first man who came through the door really wasn't that bad, after all. Over the next week, Velsa endured a parade of men.

The easiest visitors were younger men, naive and curious, with no intention to buy. Usually they came from smaller towns and considered it a novelty to spend their evening with Fanarlem girls. They stared with wide eyes, but they were too nervous to touch. Older variants of the curious man were not so naive. They were businesslike in their visits. They mostly just wanted to stare, to say that they had seen Fanarlem concubines.

The men who truly fit the description of "skarnwen", and preferred Fanarlem girls over any others, were easy to spot. Some even declared their preference openly, as if the girls might be flattered. They spoke with the assumption that the girls would want to belong to them.

One of them cornered Velsa by the window and took her hand. She felt as rigid and fragile as glass, with her small hand

10

engulfed by his. "You're so beautiful, darling," he said. "I would give anything to have you but my wife wouldn't approve. She'd be jealous. She doesn't understand that you're very different from a wife. You're something special."

Very different from a wife. Did he think this a compliment? If she were a wife, she might be forced into a marriage, but at least she would have rights.

She said nothing as he went on and on.

The next day, the weather was fine and the House was busy. They were already entertaining one shy young merchant when Dalarsha showed in a man whose eyes alighted on Velsa from her first bow. While Amleisa poured him a drink, he sat on the sofa like he owned it and held a hand out to her. "Come closer, doll, don't be scared."

They always said that. *Don't be scared.*

Nothing good ever followed those words.

She sat on the sofa beside him, rigid with fear, but it only seemed to stir him to move closer.

"Shy," he murmured, stroking her hair. "A shy little thing."

Nraya and Amleisa didn't help her this time. They sensed true danger, Velsa thought, and now it was every girl for herself.

"Don't worry," he said. "I'd treat you well. I have a beautiful house with a beautiful room that would belong to you, and every day I would bring you flowers and jewels." He produced a pair of beaded hair ornaments from his pocket. "Do you like these?"

"No," Velsa said.

"No?" He seemed affronted. "Really? Ah, you're just being shy, but no one will ever buy you if you don't relax a bit." He put a hand on her thigh and slid it up above the hem of her under-robe so that she batted him away with shock.

"Please," Velsa said. "Don't touch me. You're not allowed to touch me."

"Unless I buy you." He brought out a pouch full of coins, hefting it right before her eyes. "I could buy you and lock you away and keep you as my little pet. My secret treasure. Adorned

11

in all the finery money can buy." He put the hair ornaments in her hand and forced her fingers to close around them. Then his hand moved up her thigh again.

"*No!*" she shrieked, springing to her feet. She threw the hair ornaments at him. "*No!*"

Amleisa rushed to her side. The man was abruptly angry, red-faced, shouting, "A girl like you ought to be grateful!" Dalarsha stormed in.

"What's going on here?" she asked.

"You should teach these girls to obey," the man snapped.

"I'm very sorry, sir. We do have a policy that you must purchase them before you touch them."

The man glared at Velsa. "Then I'll buy her."

Velsa clutched Amleisa's hand. The room seemed to spin. She could not accept this. She would fight him until her limbs fell to pieces.

"Sir, I really don't think she would be a good buy for you," Dalarsha said. "Let me show you to one of the other rooms." She ushered him out, but he still gave Velsa one last look. If he insisted, what would Dalarsha do? Amleisa showed Velsa to the sofa, where she sank on shaking knees. She wanted to cry but sobs wouldn't come.

"They get like that sometimes," Amleisa said. "It's usually better to take the tips and let them touch."

"I couldn't," Velsa said. "I can't."

"It gets easier."

"No!"

"One day, you'll be bought and you won't be able to refuse. Velsa, you need to learn submission before the fight destroys you. Do you think some nice man is going to show up and rescue you?"

Surely...it isn't impossible. Amleisa is just bitter. She's been in the front of the House for almost nine months.

Nraya stood near the drinks, biting her finger.

"What truly nice man is ever going to show up here?" Amleisa said. "I think the idea that it ever happens is a myth. Men

12

buy us because we're the only woman they can own completely. They can even sew our mouths shut. We're not going to see a nice man. None of us. It's our penance. We might as well stop dreaming."

"It's all we have," Nraya said. "Dreaming."

"No," Amleisa said. "All we have is to embrace our fate. We have to accept what we are. We'll go mad if we fight. If we give our will over to our master, maybe it isn't so bad."

"*You're* mad," Velsa said. "If you think it's easier to let a man lock you up forever and treat you like a pet than it is to fight."

"Isn't it?" Amleisa spoke sadly, as if she didn't expect an answer.

Dalarsha returned, and motioned for Velsa to come with her, leading the way to her office. She waved for Velsa to sit in the rickety wooden chair opposite her cluttered desk.

"Velsa," Dalarsha said, still standing. "You know you aren't supposed to yell *at* the men. If he touches your maidenhood, you must calmly call my name, but we don't want to have a reputation that our girls are troublemakers."

Velsa stared at a row of carved wooden figurines on Dalarsha's desk, depicting Fanarlem concubines in costumes from the Age of Kings. They were all in dancing poses, with impossibly tiny feet and alluring little painted faces. They mocked her. *Why can't you be more like a figurine, Velsa?* She imagined these perfect wooden girls would be happy to be locked away.

Dalarsha put a hand on her chin. "Velsa, I don't want to see you still here in a year, because you are too rebellious."

"I'm not rebellious."

"You're the most dangerous kind of rebellious. Restrained enough that you never break the rules, but your eyes suggest that when you do, it will be in a spectacular fashion." Dalarsha smiled faintly. "I can't blame you, dear, but you have to try harder."

"Yes, madam…"

"If you yell directly at a customer again, I will have to strip your hands for a few days, but since this was the first time, I'll let it go."

In truth, serious buyers didn't come often. Besides that Fanarlem girls were expensive, they were a commitment and not to everyone's taste. Velsa was there for ten days before Dalarsha sent one to see the Village Girls.

She could tell something was different about him from the start, because Dalarsha seemed serious, and when they bowed to him, he didn't seem interested in flirting. He looked them over head to toe and made a small "hmm" sound.

"I like the look of this one," he said, pointing at Nraya.

Nraya stared at him, her face drained of its usual flirtatious smile.

"You could take some time with her, if you like," Dalarsha said.

"Yes," he said.

Dalarsha beckoned Nraya to follow her out of the room.

Velsa sank onto the sofa, her mind a swirl of emotions. *Thank the fates he didn't like the look of me.* She felt guilty for thinking it, but he might come back and decide he did like the look of her after all, and Nraya would think the same.

He hadn't waited for them to say a single word. He was seeking a 'look' and he seemed to know just what it was. What could that even mean? They had no say in how they looked.

She twisted her fingers. Every moment seemed endless.

If he chose Nraya they might never see her again.

Amleisa stood by the window, quiet. They waited as if they had breath to hold.

Half an hour later, Nraya returned with dull eyes. The man followed, with Dalarsha just behind him. "Amleisa," she said. "He'd like to see you, now."

"Yes, madam," Amleisa said, keeping her eyes down.

I might be next, Velsa thought. She got to her feet. "What happened?" she asked Nraya.

"Not all that much," Nraya said. "Dalarsha talked me up as best she could. He asked to see me without my clothes."

14

"Without your clothes?" Velsa said, dismayed.

"Yes, but when I took them off, he barely even looked. She wouldn't let him touch. He didn't say much. He just shook his head at the end... I don't know what he wanted."

The wait continued until Dalarsha returned alone.

"Amleisa has been purchased," she said gently.

"She has?" Nraya clutched her chest.

"Yes, he found her quite charming. She's been here a long time, you know. She's hungry to move on, and sometimes that's how it needs to be."

"We don't even get to say goodbye?" Velsa asked, but she already knew the answer.

Dalarsha just shook her head.

CHAPTER TWO

Outside, it was raining again. Autumn brought many days of cold drizzle, when the house seemed dim and cheerless. It almost never snowed in Nisa; it simply rained and rained. They weren't allowed any fires in the hearth until the men came; fuel was wasted on Fanarlem girls. Water lashed the windows, the trails of drizzle gleaming in the lamplight. Business would be slow again. They went an hour without any visitors at all.

Finally, the door opened. Dalarsha greeted a man downstairs. Velsa, Nraya and another girl new to the House, Lasia, stood in the hall listening. So did some of the girls from other rooms. They were all so bored. Dalarsha didn't allow them to read or embroider or do much of anything during business hours. Needlework was not seductive.

"Let me take your coat," Dalarsha told the man.

"Thank you. I'm here to buy." He added, "Maybe, if I see someone that interests me."

"And I'm sure you will," Dalarsha said. "We have wonderful girls here. The best Perfumed Ribbons in all the world." The word 'perfume' was often a euphemism for high-brow prostitutes. Flesh and blood courtesans were "Perfume Women", but Fanarlem girls were referred to as "Perfumed Ribbons", perhaps because both were fine and frivolous things made of cloth. "What kind of girl strikes your fancy?" she continued.

"Hmm," he said. "Well, let's see them all. That's too big of a decision to make without knowing all the options."

"Of course!" she said. "And a fine night for it. Not many men are braving this weather. They'll all be happy for a visitor."

She started leading him up the stairs. The girls ducked back behind their doors.

"I've never bedded with a Fanarlem girl before," he said as they reached the top of the stairs.

So he was one of the curious ones. Young-sounding. Well-bred and mannered, she thought, choosing a polite word like 'bedded' over some of the other options. His voice was respectfully soft, but direct.

Velsa doubted he would buy today. Not if he had never slept with a Fanarlem girl before. Usually the ones who bought knew what they were getting into. It was cheap enough to visit a prostitute first, to test the experience.

"Well, they have everything you need," Dalarsha said in a conspiratorial tone. "And besides that, they are very clean. Their skin is treated with spells to give them a life-like property, with special attention paid to their faces and mouths, their hands, which are all water-proofed, as well as their maidenhood, which is also given a vanishing spell so you will not have any messes after you enjoy her. They are dry, however, so oils are recommended. But I never hear any complaints. I'm sure you are aware, they are entirely adaptable. If you see a girl you like but something isn't quite to your taste, remember that you can always change any part of her body except for her eyes. The girls here are all a basic type, to keep our costs reasonable, but many nice customizations cost just a little more. I can recommend a man in town who works very quickly if you're traveling."

Velsa bit her lip. She really should never listen in on Dalarsha and the men. She didn't need detailed reminders of what a man really wanted her for, and especially that her body could be changed on his whim.

Dalarsha and the man disappeared behind a door. She heard a flurry of excited greetings from the entertainer girls.

Dalarsha must have pegged him for the sort of man who would like conversation and talent.

Velsa still wished she had been placed there. Just because she couldn't play an instrument all that well! It wasn't fair that she was left out of meeting the most thoughtful men for the sake of a few damned strings.

Velsa paced the room while Nraya and Lasia whispered the same things she had been thinking. "He won't really buy anyone today. Not if he's never been with one of us before…"

He stayed with the entertainer girls for a quarter of an hour or so, and then Dalarsha took him to the innocents. They knew very well the sound of each door.

"We always get the good ones last," Nraya said.

Lasia picked at a loose thread circling her wrist and sighed when the length of it came out, leaving a gap in her skin. "Well, he won't want me anyway, apparently I'm falling apart tonight."

"Why is that?" Velsa asked. "Why do we get the worst of it? I feel like I've done everything I'm supposed to do."

"We just don't do it well enough," Nraya said. "We're too *normal*. That's what Dalarsha told me. Men don't come here to buy someone like the girls they grew up with. Maybe we read too much."

The girls were encouraged to read. If the books in the House library were not moral tales, they were non-fiction that would enable them to have interesting conversation if the need arose. Velsa read them all a few times over.

Lasia flopped into a chair, hiding her injured wrist behind her over-robe. "Surely somewhere in the world, there must be a man who likes girls who read."

"Not for a Fanarlem concubine," Nraya said. "Maybe for a wife."

Thinking back on all the men Velsa had encountered in the past two weeks, would she have wanted to go home with a single one of them?

She twisted her hands.

"Watch it," Nraya said. "Don't you break your fingers now.

I don't think he's pulled anyone aside yet. Let's make a good impression."

Finally, almost an hour later, their door opened.

"Watch your step, sir," Dalarsha said, showing the man in. He was tall, dressed in a long black coat with red trim and silver clasps, paired with knee high boots, characteristic of any well-to-do man of the province. His black hair was in a braid down his back but he had done nothing fussy with it as many men did, such as braiding it around a wire to form a loop or wearing hair ornaments above his ears, which was currently in fashion for both men and women—Velsa had shimmering shards of abalone pinned above her ears today. His messy bangs looked like they hadn't seen a brush all day. As Velsa had guessed, he looked young, but with an air of assurance.

The three of them bowed and greeted him in unison.

He laughed faintly. "I've never been bowed to so often."

"Yes, sir, my girls are very polite. And these three, well, you will enjoy their company very much. They're well rounded and I'm sure any one of them would make a perfect companion on your journey."

A journey.

Velsa had always supposed that when she was acquired, she would be taken to a rich man's house, and given a room or two to be her home for the rest of her days, except when he took her out. Usually at night, to seedy places where concubines were welcome. It would be very much like the House of Perfumed Ribbons.

A journey…that was something new.

Something she hardly dared dream of.

He looked at her, seeming to notice how this idea had captured her attention. For a moment, their eyes met. His eyes were light brown and slanted slightly, indicating eastern blood, and making him seem a little cat-like. He was tanned, like a ship captain, like he had been on many journeys before.

"You wear a golden band," he said, his eyes moving down from her eyes to her neck. "A telepath?"

19

"It's just for precaution," Dalarsha assured him. "She has never used her abilities. The band has locked them since her creation."

"But the band could be removed?"

"Of course, if you trust her you can certainly remove it. You'll get the key when you buy her."

Velsa's tongue was stuck to the roof of her mouth. She suddenly realized her mouth was slightly open. She must have had a very startled, stupid expression.

"Can I spend a little time alone with her?" he asked. His tone was low and the rain hammering the roof made everything within the walls seem especially quiet.

"Yes, certainly!" Dalarsha sounded faintly excited. "I must chaperone you, but you can inspect her apart from the other girls, certainly."

He nodded. "I'd like to speak to her, then."

Her first inspection. Her first. Maybe her last.

Dalarsha's eyes were bright with the prospect of a potential sale. "Come, then, Velsa."

"Velsa," he said, his faint accent relishing the "l" for a moment.

Would he ask her to strip naked? Fanarlem girls never had to be naked; they never had to bathe. She wasn't used to the sight of her own skin, much less under a stranger's gaze.

Velsa forced her feet to move.

"It is a lovely name, isn't it?" Dalarsha agreed. Velsa knew Dalarsha was not just pleased because she might have money in her pocket on a cold, rainy night, but because she liked Velsa and would surely feel this man might make a good master. Still, it was strange to hear Dalarsha sounding happy to see her go.

Every part of this seemed so strange, even though she was supposed to be prepared.

Dalarsha let them all into the small private room. She offered the man a chair in one corner of the room and indicated for Velsa to stand in the center of the rug.

"Please let me know what you need to see, rather than

touching her yourself," Dalarsha said firmly.

Velsa was shivering.

"I think I can see enough from here," he said. "I'll take your word for it about the rest."

Dalarsha laughed and removed herself to the other corner of the room. The man was still standing.

"My name is Grau," he said.

"Grau." She repeated it, unable to say anything more. She was so high-strung right now, so hopeful and terrified all at once.

"In a couple of months I'll be heading north to the border to join the patrol. I would take you with me. I'm not sure where I'll go from there. I travel a lot, and I don't know when I'll settle. The conditions might be rough at times."

Dalarsha interrupted, "I'm sure you're aware that our girls are perfect for such conditions. She will not need food, drink, or baths, and she will not be prone to discomfort. Although I do caution against getting her too wet. It tends to put stuffing out of shape. There is occasional maintenance, of course, but she should be all right for months at a time if you aren't too rough with her. For practical reasons I would really not advise pulling her hair."

"Uh, no," he said, looking as if he might also prefer if she stopped talking. Then he looked at Velsa again. "You would see a lot of the country. I have no intention of marrying—no Daramon girl would put up with this life—so you would be my only girl."

She had seen more handsome men. A Daramon men wealthy enough to afford a Fanarlem concubine was also wealthy enough for shape-shifting, but she didn't think his face had ever been shape-shifted. He looked like he squinted into the sun a lot; if he cared for fashion he would have wanted his eyes to seem larger. Nor did he sound like the wealthiest man she would meet. But there was something earnest in his manner that made her hope and pray that he would value her companionship.

At least she wouldn't be locked away as someone's prisoner. "I would like to go, sir," she said. "Very much."

He looked at her face so carefully that she felt a shudder down her spine, because she was sure that look meant he would say yes. Or he would say no. He would say something and she was equally terrified of each option.

He drew back and nodded decisively. "I will take her."

"Oh, wonderful, sir. Very good choice. You won't regret it for a moment. Velsa is a personal favorite of mine. I thought, from the moment I saw you, that she might be a good choice for you."

What a lie, Velsa thought. *She showed me to him last!* Unless that was a tactic. The best for last. She hated to believe the worst of Dalarsha, even now. Dalarsha was the closest thing she had to a parent.

He took out a money purse. "Two hundred and twenty ilan, is it?"

"That's right."

He poured out the contents of the bag. Her price, already counted. He gave the money to Dalarsha.

She took a small bag from a nearby cabinet and handed it to him. "There are some things to go with her, for minor repairs, some oils and whatnot..." She fished out a small gold wand, the size of a pen. "And this is the key to her golden band. She is yours now."

Dalarsha came over to Velsa and embraced her. "I'm so glad, my dear. I think you've found a good home."

"Do you have anyone to say goodbye to? Anything of your own to take with you?" Grau asked.

"She does not," Dalarsha said. "All she needs is you, sir."

Of course she owned things, had friends to bid goodbye. Of course.

But Dalarsha and their other teachers said they couldn't take anything. She had to pretend she was newly born in this moment.

He was looking at her, and his brow furrowed. "Surely she could take a memento. I'll pay for it."

He seemed to think that Dalarsha was forbidding her from taking anything from the House, when in fact the rule was for his benefit.

22

Dalarsha looked even happier. "You are too kind, sir. Velsa…if you would like to take something from your room, it sounds as if Mr. Thanneau won't mind."

"Of course I don't mind," he said. "I've got this much space in my bag." He framed a shape with his hands. "It's all right if you want to take some time to say goodbye to your friends."

She rushed from the room, almost tripping on her own feet. Fanarlem were by nature a little clumsy anyway, and she was so startled she didn't so much walk down the hall as flail, veering toward the wall. The other girls were gathered nearby and they erupted with questions when they saw her.

"He said no?"

"What happened?"

"He bought me," Velsa said. "He told me to bring something with me and—and say goodbye."

Pia gasped. "Oh, he's very good then!"

"You lucky girl!" Nraya cried.

They were all grabbing her, hugging her, tugging on her hair to hassle her for such good fortune—Dalarsha would not approve. She was sobbing on the inside, but on the outside she was completely quiet. Relief mingled with a despair that threatened to overwhelm her.

She went down the dim halls in the back of the House to her room. The only light here at this time was normally the moon, and due to the rain, she had to fumble around the beds to the shelf where the girls kept their few possessions. She found her precious wooden box and clutched it against her. She should be happy he was allowing her to take the one thing that really felt like hers, but right now it felt stupid. No better than bringing toys.

Even if he was kind enough, she was aware of a cold fact. She didn't want to belong to any man who was willing to take a pile of valuable coins down to a place like this, on a night like this, and buy a woman for his own pleasure.

CHAPTER THREE

Dalarsha wrapped her in a wool cloak and exchanged her slippers for sturdy boots. The door opened to the cold, wet darkness. Grau had a hand wrapped lightly around her shoulders, steering her toward a horse standing under the edge of the roof.

The door shut behind her.

This was her life now.

The horse was untethered. She wondered if the saddle was enchanted to keep the horse in place and deter thieves. She had heard of this but it seemed like expensive magic. At least he was not too poor, then. Some men scrimped and saved for a Fanarlem girl but had little else to offer.

"I can pack that away," he said, offering a hand to take her box.

"Thank you."

"Wow, that's heavy. What's in here?" He opened the box, without asking. Revealing all of her rocks and nut husks and other odds and ends. "What are these?" he asked.

"Nothing, sir."

He looked at her uncertainly and shut the box again. Her heart sank. Maybe he expected her to have a more romantic possession. Maybe he didn't want to carry a box of rocks.

"The rain is very loud," he said. "Can I lift you onto the horse?"

"Yes," she said, relieved that at least he had not left the box behind.

He put his hands around her waist to lift her up.

"Oof," he said. "You're heavy too." Although he had no trouble putting her up on the saddle.

"Am I?" She had always felt fairly insubstantial.

"I guess you weigh a little less than a flesh and blood woman. Maybe. It's not a bad thing, though. Wouldn't want to lose you in a strong wind." He swung up behind her. He took the reins, his arms close around her. His body was warm against her back. Often she was disturbed by the warmth of men, but on a night like this, it wasn't so unwelcome. She couldn't get cold the way real people did, but cold weather still didn't feel good, especially wet cold like this. She could feel the damp in her wooden bones.

He took a white stone from his pocket and tapped it twice. It brightened like a lantern, and he held it up to cast the way ahead, but barely. They moved slowly down the streets, pelted by rain. Her hooded cloak protected her, but he also kept his head tipped forward over hers. She was deeply conscious of how his body pressed around her, the muscles of his thighs, the size of him. Fanarlem girls were all made the same, five feet tall, so their parts could be easily changed without worrying over size. Besides that, they became clumsier the larger their bodies were made. Grau was perhaps six feet, not unusually tall, but she had never been this close to a man—as close as an embrace. Very different from perching reluctantly on a man's knee.

She wasn't sure how long they traveled down the liquid shadows of those wet streets. She was so aware of him near her and so uncertain of what might come next, time seemed a tricky concept. They went far enough to leave the seedy district of the House of Perfumed Ribbons well behind them, now traveling on a tree-lined avenue near the river where wealthy merchants must live in the elegant stone houses. The river wove its way across the land to the port of Atlantis in the south, all the way to the Miralem lands in the north. Sometimes people called it the River of Money.

He stopped in front of a small but cozy-looking inn, two stories with a balcony and a tiled roof, where candles glowed in windows. A boy walked out from the stables into the rain to take the horse. He looked at Velsa.

"Success, huh?" he asked.

"I'd say so," Grau replied.

Grau removed her box and some papers from his bag. Then he lifted her down and showed her to the steps, fishing out a key as he climbed.

The room was small but they had it to themselves. There was a single large bed on a low frame. Seeing it twisted her insides. Also, a lounging bench with cushions, a writing desk, a fireplace. Grau put her box on the bed, took off his coat and hung it on a peg. He offered a hand to take her cloak.

"You aren't wet, are you?" he asked.

"No, sir."

"Please, call me Grau," he said.

"All right…"

He shivered, ruffling his black hair, which was soaking wet as he didn't have a hood. "I'll get the fire going. Have a seat."

She watched him move the logs around and stuff some paper beneath them. He put his hand close to the logs, blew out a quick jet of breath, and a flame sprouted.

Magic. Just small magic, but magic all the same. She had never seen anyone work sorcery right before her eyes.

Once he was satisfied that the fire would burn steadily, he sat beside her with her box on his lap. "Where did you get these?" he asked.

Fates, how she was shaking! "Once a year…" She could hardly get her voice to go above a whisper. "…when the city is hot in the dead of summer and the mosquitos are out, so no one is coming to the House, we go to the mountains for a week. I always pick up interesting things I see, to remind me what it's like out in the forest."

"I would love to look at them closer."

"Of—of course."

26

He opened the box and at first, he just looked at all the contents long and hard without touching anything. Then, slowly, he held his hand over the box, as if he was sensing something inside. He picked up one of the rocks and turned it over. "A fossil," he said, noticing the imprint of a shell inside the rock. "You have a good eye."

"Is that what you call it?"

"It's a remnant from a time when the mountains were an ocean," he said. "A long time ago."

"How?" She briefly shed her fear enough to question. She had always wondered how a shell could have ever been atop a mountain.

"No one knows," he said. "But sorcerers who study these things report sensing the energy of ocean creatures in the mountains, and of course, we find things like this. Maybe ancient sorcerers moved the land around."

He took a little glass out and squinted into it.

"What is that?" she asked.

"A magnifier. Here, take a look."

The magnifier made the shell seem almost like the surface of another world. "Why do you carry that around?" she asked.

"For just this reason. Looking at things. Sorcerers use things in the natural world to create spells, but so much of it remains a mystery. The best way to find a new spell is to study how nature works. How all the components of our world fit together and work in harmony. Sometimes, if you apply those same combinations and processes to spell-work, you'll get something new and wonderful."

"So you're a sorcerer?"

"I won't really feel like a sorcerer until I discover a spell of my own."

"I didn't realize sorcerers had to discover a spell."

"They don't, but…it's the best way to make a name for yourself. Either way, I can't pursue sorcery as a profession until I improve my potion-making skills. That's where the money is."

"But for now, you'll be joining the military?"

27

"Just the border patrol, for six months. I have three older brothers, and we've all been working for my father, but being the youngest I have the dregs of the inheritance. I need to do something with myself besides overseeing our shipments. This will get me out into the world."

The fire was crackling and burning now, giving the room a warm glow. "And you bought me to accompany you during your military service? Is that common?"

"My father was a soldier once. He said if I was going into the border patrol, all the other men on the patrol would surely be seeking female company in town, and I might be tempted to join them," he said. "But it's perilous nowadays. Miralem women can sneak in over the border and use their telepathy to steal everything a man's got. There are reports of men waking up from a stupor with their eyes cut out, and worse."

Even in her sheltered life, Velsa heard plenty of talk about the Miralem people who lived in the northern regions. They were all born with telepathy, and the more talented among them could read and control minds.

"I suppose it's their contribution to the war effort," Grau continued.

"War? We aren't at war, are we?"

"We could be, any minute. It's all anyone talks about at home." He shrugged. "So this was all his idea. You, I mean. I really don't know that I'd visit brothels, but then, I also don't know how long I'll be traveling around. It could be years and years. It does get lonely." He regarded her, his expression turning more serious. "I've always been told that Fanarlem don't have emotions like real people do, but it isn't true, is it? The way you look at me…"

"Of course we have emotions," Velsa said, offended. "All the girls do."

"It's making me feel a little uncomfortable that I bought you."

"I've heard people say that about us…" Velsa plucked at the hem of her sleeve. "Some men don't like to buy such well-made Fanarlem with education. Too much like a real girl…but, I am still a Fanarlem."

At this point, Velsa knew, she should assure him that she was happy to do anything he asked of her, that she was his willing servant because it would cleanse her tainted soul. But some rebellious part of her never liked to voice those sentiments, and she even now she couldn't bring herself to do it.

"I understand that your karma is improved by obedience," he said. "But I think I'd have a hard time asking you to do something you didn't want to do."

She glanced at him. She feared it almost came across as a glare, and looked at her hands again. "I would be happy to do anything you ask," she said softly.

He shifted a little closer to her. "You really are astonishing magic," he said. "When you consider that we ever figured out how to host a living soul inside a shell of wood and cloth, and make it so you can speak and move… You are so much more luminous than the sum of your parts."

She had been prepared for this her whole life, in the sense that she was told it was coming. She was told what men would want to do to her and what they would want her to do to them, what she should say and not say. But he was entirely new to her. Every thought had left her head, except his body so near her, the soft brown of his eyes with the gleam of the fire in them, the ghost of stubble on his chin.

"Magic I could hold in my arms," he said. "That's what I imagined. I can sense the spells woven through you. Can you sense them?"

"Can I sense them?" She hadn't expected that question. "No."

"You could, with some training," he said. "It's very interesting. I've never sensed so many layers of magic at once."

Slowly, his hands moved to her shoulders. She didn't move or protest. She wasn't sure what she wanted, exactly. She had been so terrified with every other man at the House, but he didn't behave like the other men.

29

He put his hands on her over-robe and gently slid it off her shoulders, revealing the curve of her narrow waist hugged by her sash, a glimpse of bare thighs between stockings and under-robe. All the stitches at her joints were still concealed by her clothes. She had been told some men liked to see them and some did not.

Grau looked at her, and she could see he was intrigued. She had seen that look before, of course. Hunger in his eyes. Men went about their lives all day, conducting business and working, but if given a chance, they were like wolves.

She braced herself. This was the moment she had been created for. All she had to do was let him have what he wanted. Stare at the ceiling, Pia had told her breezily. Easy for Pia to say, when she'd spent time with Fanarlem men and apparently liked it, but real men seemed so different.

Grau met her eyes again, and he seemed concerned.

"You look scared," he said.

She shook her head.

It would be perilous to take his concern at face value and rebuff him. She could not forget that he had spent a tidy sum on her.

She unfastened her sash, letting her under-robe fall open, and then she slid the garment off entirely so now he would see the stitches at her wrists and elbows and shoulders, the curve of her small breasts under the thin fabric of her chemise.

He put his hand on her arm. His motions were careful, as if he thought she was made of glass. She tried to stay calm. No one had ever really cared, or ever really would care, if she could play the bastir or make conversation. This was all that mattered.

"You *are* scared," he said, drawing back again. "You are a real woman, with feelings, and you're frightened of me..."

"No."

"I think this was a mistake."

He might send her back.

A surge of desperation and unexpected horror ran down her body. She knew in this moment that she couldn't bear the uncertainty of that place ever again.

"Grau, please, don't think of it like that! You think I'd be any less scared with someone else? I *wanted* you to acquire me."

His hand wrapped around his mouth, thinking. "You just aren't anything like I expected you'd be. And now that I'm considering this entire situation, I must have been out of my mind. My father made it sound like I'd just go pick out a girl who would be as willing to spend her life with me as our servants are to scrub the dishes. But this is a very different circumstance, isn't it? When I looked in your eyes I wasn't thinking of any of that. I suppose I imagined I was rescuing you."

"You were." She put her hand on his chest. His heart beat under her fingers. She didn't expect that, and almost jumped. "Grau..."

"Velsa..." He spoke her name so intimately. He took her hand and looked at it carefully, running his finger along the tops of her fingernails, which were crafted from finely carved slivers of horn. "I wanted to rescue you. Maybe it's true about Fanarlem. That's what I've always been told. But being here with you now... I can't treat you that way. I won't touch you."

Until you're ready.

She heard words unspoken. She knew he must assume the day would come when she would be ready. Even marriages were usually arranged, wives not necessarily any more willing than she was. She wondered how long he would wait.

She wondered if she wanted him to wait. Maybe it was better to get it over with.

And yet, she nodded, relief flooding through her.

"You look tired," he said. "Maybe you should sleep." He waved toward the bed. "It's big enough for two. I'm going to look over some work papers before I turn in. I won't bother you when I do."

"It's—it's fine." She hurried over to the bed, wearing just her chemise and stockings because she couldn't very well sleep in robes; they would tangle around her. She ducked under the covers, relieved to be concealed—but at some point he would be beside her.

31

She didn't know how she would sleep, although suddenly she was very tired. She really hadn't slept well since she moved to the front of the House.

"Comfortable?" he asked.

"Yes." It was actually rather nice, with the room warmed by the fire as the rain hammered the tile roof above. She wasn't used to being warm on a cold night.

"Sleep well. We're in no rush to leave early tomorrow." He took out his papers and held the magic light up to them. She watched him for a moment, in the room's soft glow, as he looked over papers that were crumpled from travel and smoothed back his wild hair.

"What work are you doing now?" she murmured.

"My family raises freshwater fish," he said. "We farm it in a lake, pack it on ice and ship it to Atlantis, where it's considered a delicacy. They have all the ocean fish they could want, so they pay more for freshwater fish. Typical, isn't it? The ocean fish tastes better."

"Don't you think that because you grew up with the freshwater kind?"

He laughed. "No. My opinions about fish are surely irrefutable."

She fell asleep without hardly realizing it, and woke when he climbed under the covers, keeping to the opposite edge of the bed. She thought she would be disturbed to have him there, but instead the heat of his body and the slow, steady sound of his breath felt like something she remembered. She dared to sniff him gently. He smelled a little like smoke and a little like horse, and maybe a little like man—but not in a bad way.

She recalled the beat of his heart, the flutter of life beneath her touch, and had an impulse to touch his chest again. Instead, she curled her hands against her own still body, and resisted the urge to draw closer to his warmth.

CHAPTER FOUR

She woke to morning sunshine. Grau was stirring a pot on the fireplace.

"Would you like any breakfast?" he asked.

"I can't eat."

"Oh. Of course. I wasn't thinking."

She pulled on her clothes and realized she didn't even own a comb now. The girls left with only the clothes on their back; everything else was their new owner's responsibility.

"I have a comb by the washstand," Grau said, when he saw her fingers messing with her locks.

She stepped into the small room, which had a basin of water and a small mirror, and a lidded pot on the floor for flesh and blood people to do their business. An unpleasant reminder that Grau was a real man, and the girls in training were always warned to try and hide any revulsion they might feel from a real man, with all their sweating and digestion.

At least Grau seemed like he kept clean. He had obviously already been here to wash up this morning and comb his own hair. Last night he looked a little wild, but it was the end of a rainy day. She carefully combed the sleep tangles from her own thick black hair—always trying to lose as few strands as possible —while regarding herself in the mirror. She looked the same as ever: big golden eyes with thick lashes, a perfectly shaped red mouth with ever-so-slightly turned up corners so her expression always had the vague suggestion of a mysterious smile. The girls' faces had been made so they looked youthful but knowing, and seductive even without trying. In some strange way, Velsa felt this made life easier, because when she looked in the mirror she saw a girl who looked like she knew what she was doing, and this made her believe it might be true.

Grau was spooning rice into a bowl. "I feel so inhospitable eating while you do nothing."

"I don't mind."

"Wherever you go in this country, it's all people do. They feed you and they pour you drinks. We don't even know what to do with ourselves otherwise." He cracked a raw egg on top of his rice and garnished it all with some herbs and salt. "Can you taste?"

"I can, but it really doesn't matter. That food doesn't look too appealing anyway."

He laughed. "I just wonder why you wouldn't be able to eat. If you can speak, why not eat?"

"I suppose I *could* eat, if I spit everything out when I was done. The food has to go somewhere."

"There must be some magic to allow it. If you already have a vanishing spell applied...to one place." He looked a little embarrassed.

She hugged herself, embarrassed too. "I really don't need to eat. It would cost you money and the food would go to waste."

"Hmm. Perhaps, but it seems almost criminal not to enjoy food."

When they left the inn, he asked her lots of questions about her life at the House.

"So you were only for sale for two weeks before I came along?"

"That's right."

"That isn't too long, then."

"It seemed like forever." Questions like that only reminded her of the immense gap between their perceptions of life. She

34

could never convey the horror of it.

"I guess you'd meet some pretty unsavory characters in there," he said.

"Yes, but they couldn't touch," she said, to reassure him that she was a maiden, as advertised.

"What did you do before? Did you go to school? Can you read?"

"I can read, yes. We had some schooling. Some of it was learning and lots of it was moral lecturing..."

"I see. About Fanarlem souls."

"Yes."

"What if it wasn't true at all?" he mused. "And you spent your entire life trying to cleanse your soul of sins you never committed?"

Velsa was silent. She had wondered this herself, in the private depths of her mind, but never heard a flesh and blood person voice the idea before. The other girls barely touched on the subject. It was not a hopeful idea. She couldn't imagine flesh and blood people would accept Fanarlem as equals.

She wasn't sure how he expected her to answer. "If it is true, and I don't accept my penance, I'll keep coming back to life as a Fanarlem over and over," she said.

"Hmm."

They had reached a crossroads, where a man was urging an oxen through the wet, rutted road. Shops with overhanging balconies crowded around a square, where a few groups of nicely dressed ladies walked with their servants, who carried their packages. Grau stopped to pull out an unwieldy map of the city, its folds so large that they draped on her lap. "Never any signs in this town," he said. "Not like Atlantis."

"You've been to Atlantis lots of times, I guess?" She had read about the capital city, and the many things to see there. Ruins of old palaces. Canals that ran beneath the streets. Tall ships in the harbor. And the world's wealthiest merchants, dealing in magic and spices and cloth by day, and by night, frequenting the gambling dens and smoky dance halls. A lot of the girls dreamed of being purchased by a merchant from Atlantis who might take them around to all the night spots and buy them the latest fashions.

"Here and there," he said. "It's a lot like Nisa, only bigger. Crowded, dirty, wet…"

"Surely it must be better than Nisa."

"Well, you're right," he said wryly. "It has signs." He clicked his tongue, urging the horse down a narrow alley. "Some people seem to enjoy it. It is certainly lavish, and perhaps more enjoyable if you have more money than you know what to do with."

Just ahead hung a sign depicting a hand with a stitched wrist and a pair of scissors.

The Fanarlem parts shop. He hadn't mentioned anything about this. Was he going to change something about her appearance?

"Wait here," he said. "Fern won't go anywhere." He patted his horse on the neck and slipped into the shop, oblivious to her distress. He had left the map with her, and she tried to distract herself by studying the maze of streets and notable buildings. Almost all of them were unfamiliar to her. The girls were rarely taken out. They might easily be snatched.

Someone could snatch her now, in fact.

She smoothed Fern's mane, a nervous gesture that the horse didn't seem to mind. The lane was empty but she remained tense. Grau hadn't brought her in with him, so he could only be making an inquiry.

A few minutes later, he walked out with a bottle and a triumphant expression. "I've got it!"

"What?"

"The spell that allows you to eat!"

"I—I thought maybe you were going to replace some of my parts."

"Certainly not." He handed the small bottle up to her. "Drink it. It'll disappear. The fellow in there said it was safe. I want to see how it works."

She opened the bottle and took a tentative sniff of the contents. It smelled much like the spirits they served the men in the House. One slow evening all the girls tasted them; swished them around in their mouths and spat them back in the bottle with no one the wiser.

She poured the contents onto her tongue.

"You have to swallow it," he said.

"Haw?" she asked, around the little pool collected in her mouth.

"Maybe…tip your head back so it gets into your throat."

She lifted her chin, and as her head craned back, the potion dropped into the passage built into her neck. It was constructed like a small pocket that ended halfway down, but now as the potion collected there, it all opened up and she had an abrupt and instinctive understanding of how to swallow the rest. It felt exactly right, and now she wondered how she had ever been able to stand having her throat closed off.

"It worked!" She put a hand to her neck, her fingers meeting the golden band. "It didn't even feel strange."

He snapped his fingers. "Now I have to get you something nice. Something *delicious*. Is there any food you've ever wanted to try?"

"Bread," she said, without even needing to think. There was a little bakery just down the road from the House. On fine days she would wake herself up by drinking in the air that smelled of fresh bread.

"That's too easy."

"I don't know much about food…"

"Then, we'll go to a nice bakery and see what we find." He climbed back on the horse, briefly putting his arm around her waist as he resettled behind her. An unfamiliar wave of feeling passed over her for just a moment—that someone was taking care of her, protecting her, delighting in her delight.

It was not without uneasiness. For all his promises, she was still a possession, and he had complete control of her destiny. He seemed to find her an intriguing novelty, but she dared not take this for granted.

They came to a cafe on a little tucked away street, where
the walls were painted yellow and the doors and window frames
were painted blue, and plants grew indoors in clay pots. Even on
a chilly autumn day, the cafe reminded her of summer. Everyone
inside seemed in a summer mood, light-hearted and festive. A
fireplace burned gently on one side of the room, where women
had shed their coats to drink cups of coffee and bask in the
warmth, laughing and chatting. At one table, another woman
shared a pastry with a little girl with blue ribbons woven through
her hair. Velsa had never been surrounded by so much ease, by
arms slung casually over chair backs, the din of conversation, the
spoons gently stirring sugar and cream into cups.

A long counter displayed dozens of pastries, cakes covered
in chopped nuts and doughy circles drenched in golden syrup.
Small glass cups filled with three different layers of cream, and
square pies of dough filled with berries.

Behind the counter, three girls with dusty aprons covering
their clothes moved with a frantic energy managing customers
and products; grabbing long loaves of bread and filling sacks with
rolls, reaching with tongs for just the right chocolate dipped fruit.

Some of the customers lingered for long moments in front
of the glass counter, puzzling over what to order, brushing off
help. Grau, meanwhile, was decisive. He asked for five different
pastries, a loaf of dark bread, and butter. One of the girls
presented them to him on a plate and it seemed to Velsa that he
paid a sizable for sum for the food, but then, she wasn't sure how
much food ought to cost.

"This one is my favorite," he said, setting the plate down at
one of the few free tables. "Raspberry tart. I went overboard
ordering. But this is a special occasion, the first meal of your life.
And I don't suppose you ever have to worry about getting too
full."

She thought she knew what taste was; like smells on the
tongue, but no, it was far more potent. She could have eaten

38

forever, as if she had a lifetime to catch up on. Each pastry was different; one was soft and buttery with a glaze of sugar, one was made of very fine layers with a nutty paste inside, one had flower petals baked into the top and tasted as delicate as it appeared.

"I told you I didn't need to eat," she said, feeling sheepish at trying them all.

"Eating is such a huge part of being alive. If I was always eating and you never were, it wouldn't feel right. You're enjoying it, aren't you?"

"I am." She ventured a smile. All of this hardly seemed real.

A man having a cup of coffee at a nearby table kept looking at them. As he stood up to go, he stopped by Grau and said, "From the House of Perfumed Ribbons, eh?"

"Yes."

"You married?"

"No, sir."

"Be smart and keep it that way. She's a beauty. And if you marry, the wife will be kicking your doll to the curb before you know it, even if she says she won't. They always get jealous. Believe me." He laughed knowingly.

Grau's responding laugh was terse. "I got Velsa precisely because I don't intend to marry."

"Hold onto that spirit. I envy you," the man continued. "To have such a pretty little creature to command for all your days, instead of the wife always telling me what to do...and getting older, too. If she keeps going to the shape-shifter, she won't have a face left, and I won't have any money."

"Hmm," Grau said. "I don't think I could show my face to my mother again if I talked about a woman that way, Velsa included."

"Ah, youth. I haven't worried about showing my face to my mother in a long time." The man chuckled, moving along.

"I feel sorry for his wife," Grau muttered.

She nodded, but the moment was soured. She didn't dare let down her guard. This was only the first day, and so many men

39

loved to indulge a concubine—at first.

"I meant to tell you earlier," Velsa said, "but you should be more careful with leaving me alone on the street. I could be kidnapped."

"You're right. Sometimes I'm absent-minded when I get an idea. I won't do it again." He looked at the remaining pieces of pastry. They had both stopped eating when the man appeared. "You're done, aren't you?"

"Yes."

Grau tucked the leftover pastries away in a waxed cloth for later. He seemed more sober now. She wondered if he was considering the fact that if he ever fell in love with a flesh and blood woman, he would have to explain her, or find somewhere else to put her.

"When we leave the city, we're going back to my family home in Marjon for a month," he said. "My father paid for you, so he'll want to see you. But you'll need more clothes. A couple of outfits suitable for mucking around in the marshland and traveling with the patrol, and a nice dress, at the least. No time to hire a dressmaker, so we'll have to stop at the used market."

The used clothing market occupied a large central square. Many of the vendor booths were permanent while others were hastily pitched tents. Even on the periphery, outside the official boundaries of the market, shabby little women spread ragged tunics and scarves onto blankets and shouted prices at passerby. It was so busy that in certain narrow spots they had to hold hands and edge around other bodies single file. Velsa was very careful not to smell the air here. She expected many of these people would fit Pia's descriptions of unwashed city folk.

All she had ever worn were the simple tunics and slim trousers of childhood, and then the robes of a concubine. She had just one outfit at a time. Their clothes almost never needed to be cleaned, because they never handled food or got near the fire. When the clothing grew shabby, they were given a new garment, much the same as the last.

In the market, styles varied widely, from all the people of

different regions who came trading along the river. Some were imported, like the beautiful embroidered Halnari sashes that were hung lengthwise along the vendor tents. Grau seemed to know what to look for and how to haggle. She could only offer an occasional opinion on what colors or fabrics she liked.

She kept trying to imagine what he meant by 'mucking around the marshlands'. Surely he didn't really mean for her to roam the outdoors. Or maybe he did. He had been so interested in her rock collection.

With all the business attended to, they resumed their journey. As night fell, they were on the outskirts of town, and stayed at another inn, not as nice as the last.

They had their evening meal downstairs in the dining room, surrounded by many dirty, calloused men who stared at Velsa, but left her alone. The same could not be said for a handsome young man in a fur-trimmed blue tunic with obsidian earrings and his hair in a neatly formed loop-braid. He sat down at their table while they were eating.

"Hey there," he said to Grau, crossing his arms on the table, displaying several jeweled rings. "You sure have a nice-looking doll. Too nice for a place like this, eh?" He jabbed a thumb at the rest of the room.

"We're fine, thanks," Grau said.

"I was just giving you a compliment. Still, I wonder if you'd consider an offer."

"No," Grau said.

"You don't know how *much* I'm offering."

"I wouldn't sell her for any price," Grau said. "She's a *girl*, not a piece of farm equipment."

"You bought her, didn't you? I'd really just like to have her for an hour. I've traveled a long while and I'm partial to Fanarlem girls myself."

Velsa had never realized that leaving the House and belonging to one man would in no way save her from every other leering man in the world. She would never be safe anywhere. At some point on Grau's travels it seemed practically inevitable that someone would steal her away from him.

The man put some coins on the table. "You could buy her a whole new untainted body for that."

"I couldn't buy her an untainted mind." Grau wolfed down the last few bites of his stew and gave Velsa's elbow a small tug toward the door.

Apparently, they were leaving.

The man followed them, shoving past a half-drunk crowd near the bar. Just outside the door, he caught Velsa's hand and tried to yank her toward him. Grau seized her other hand. She imagined them tearing her in two.

"Hey," the man said. "I don't appreciate your tone. I'm making you an offer that is more than fair. She's just a Fanarlem and I like the look of her. Your mother never taught you to share your toys?"

"Let go of her." Grau spoke with deadly calm. "She's precious to me."

"Pampered little snot." The man shoved Velsa at Grau, and she stumbled. She would have fallen if he hadn't caught her. He held her close. His breathing was quick.

Grau waved his hand toward the lantern burning outside of the inn and then swept his fingers back toward his body. Flame sprung up in the palm of his hand.

Velsa stepped back. Fire frightened her. The stories she read at the House often ended with a disobedient, willful Fanarlem being burned to death, screaming with pain until the eye that held their soul finally melted away.

"Oh, a bit of sorcery." The man's tone was scathing. He twisted one of the rings on his fingers. Grau flung the flame at him, scorching his sleeve, as a bolt of blue magic, so bright it hurt her eyes, shot from the ring.

Grau clutched his stomach, but at the same time he stepped forward, holding up his hands as if he intended to strangle the man.

Grau sucked in a long breath of air, weaving his fingers as if he was drawing from the other man's lungs.

The man choked. He shook his head and his arms twitched and waved in what seemed to be a gesture of surrender.

Grau exhaled forcefully, and the man coughed.

"Parlor tricks," he spat.

"I have plenty more, if you're enjoying them," Grau said.

The man ducked into the inn door, slamming it behind him.

"That was amazing," Velsa said. "But are you hurt?"

"It'll be all right," Grau said, through gritted teeth. "Let's get out of here."

He went to the stables, still clutching his stomach.

"I never imagined, when I got you, that complete strangers would expect to have you," he said, as the stablehand readied Fern. "He wouldn't ask to take my horse out for a ride, would he? And Fern probably wouldn't even be bothered, but..."

Velsa felt as if she never wanted to see another flesh and blood person again. She knew she shouldn't feel so *angry*. Fanarlem should not be angry at real people; anger was for Grau to feel, but she had no idea how to smother her feelings on the inside, only the outside.

"Maybe you'd better put on the jacket and pants I bought you," Grau said. "That might stop it. For all they'd know, you were flesh-born."

"Flesh-born?"

"You know, like you were born a real woman."

"Is that possible?"

"It's rare, but once in a while people choose to become Fanarlem to extend their lives—if their body was badly maimed, for instance."

"Might people really think that I was flesh-born?" Velsa had never heard of this surprising possibility.

"Why not?"

She supposed what really surprised her was that he wouldn't mind people thinking she was flesh-born, because then they would surely think she was his wife, to be traveling alone with him. His status would be elevated by owning a Fanarlem

43

concubine; she suspected it would be the opposite if he had a flesh-born Fanarlem wife, who could not produce heirs.

They rode on through the darkness to the next town, finding a very shabby inn, but it was run by welcoming people who seemed happy to have another guest turning up so late.

The room was small and drafty, and the bed wasn't meant for two.

"I could sleep on the floor," Grau offered, but he was still clutching his stomach and moving carefully.

"Not with your injury! I won't find it as uncomfortable as you would. But…Grau, I don't think I would mind if we were close. I'm not sure if I would even mind if you held me. You're very warm."

"Do you get cold?"

"Not cold the way you do, but…it makes me feel safe. And I feel…very unsafe right now."

He drew close and put a hand on her shoulder. "And no wonder."

Velsa smiled wanly and then gently pulled his hand away from his tunic. The fabric was scorched in a tidy circle. And the skin beneath? She unfastened the clasps.

"This isn't how I imagined you'd undress me," he murmured.

Her face heated. Luckily a blush could not betray her.

"At least when we get to my family home," he said, "we'll be away from it all. We'll have hours and hours to roam the marshes without seeing another person. I'll teach you a bit of magic."

The attack had left a red welt on his skin, not much larger than a coin, but it looked painful.

"It's not so bad," he said. "Daramons are tough these days. My blood will heal itself."

"Because of the Ten Thousand Man Sacrifice?" A century ago, the High Sorcerer Kalan Jherin gathered ten thousand Daramons willing to sacrifice themselves for the future of their children. The blood they spilled created a spell so powerful that it enchanted the blood of all Daramons in the world, so they would heal rapidly and survive most fatal injuries. It had also extended their lifespan, from an average of ninety years, to nearly a century and a half. The High Sorcerer himself was two hundred years old, but of course he had access to the best magic the world could offer.

"Yes. You could rip out my heart and sew it back in half an hour later and I'd probably survive."

"Still, some medicine wouldn't hurt, if you have any." She had picked up a few things from talking to the Little Wives.

"The little green bottle in my bag."

He sat down on the bed while she found the medicine. He pressed his shirt against the wound. It didn't seem as if touching the welt would feel better, but obviously it did. What did she know of wounds?

She opened the jar and scooped out a dab of medicine, smelling the sharp herbal aroma before dabbing it on his skin. The wound immediately lost some of its angry red color.

Grau watched her with the same serious expression as the first moment they met.

Her hand moved, as if his eyes were a magnet that drew her hands forward. She placed her palm on his chest, to feel his own heartbeat again. The gentle flutter of it seemed too vulnerable, to give power to his long, solid legs and the hands that lifted her so easily. It gave her a pang, to think of how fragile he really was, how many parts of him could be hurt, and yet he didn't even seem to consider that most of the time. He was so much stronger than her. It must make him feel very confident.

He kept gently studying her face for a moment. His eyes said so much, it was hard not to trust him, even though she didn't dare trust anyone entirely. He was fascinated with her. She could see it all there.

Certainly, he was not the first man to look at her with fascination. But it was different, with Grau. His expression had a weight that went beyond mere curiosity or desire. She felt like he was searching out her soul. She couldn't look away.

He finally did, leaning forward to unbutton his boots.

She took off her robes, feeling a little shy as she climbed into bed beside him. He faced away from her, but on the small mattress, their bodies touched. The wool she was stuffed with warmed immediately against him and she reflected that once all that wool had been the coat of a living creature, and her bones had been the body of a living tree.

"Grau," she said. "When you're awake and I'm sleeping, does it feel like being next to a living person?"

"Yes," he said. "It certainly does. Even when you're sleeping, and very still, I sense the magic that gives you life."

"How does it feel?"

"A little bit electric," he said. "A little bit like a heartbeat, almost." He turned onto his back so he could meet her eyes. "You are certainly alive."

"I'm conscious," she said. "And moving. But I mean more than that. I mean feeling like I have a body and not just a shell. Like I belong here."

He gently brushed back the hair that was falling across her cheek. "To me, you feel vibrantly alive," he said. "You were created differently, but that's all right. Lots of things are. Some creatures are born from wombs, some hatch out of eggs, some are spun from magic."

She rested her head against his shoulder, and he slipped an arm around her back. The warmth was so delicious, it almost made her shiver.

She wanted more of him.

More of his warmth, more of his strength, more of the way he looked at her.

She still feared him, too. She could hardly voice the reasons why, when he had treated her so well.

Only, there seemed to be no point in resisting her feelings. She should count herself lucky that she was starting to feel a true attraction to the man who had chosen her. Even if he broke her heart, she would have nowhere better to go…wasn't that obvious enough already? She wouldn't be safe anywhere, much less free.

It's my fault, she thought. *I always did everything I was supposed to do, but Dalarsha still made me a Village Girl. I'm not obedient. I don't want to be anyone's possession, not even Grau's, even it means my soul is cursed...*

In the morning, he was already out of bed when she woke. He seemed to like mornings more than she did. She marveled that he hadn't tried to touch her in the night, after she had chosen to stay so close to him. Their instruction at the House had never suggested men had much patience.

He handed her a folded pile of clothes. Pants of sturdy black cotton; a short tunic with a plain sash, a high collar that concealed the golden band, and long cuffed sleeves; a black hat with flaps to shield one's ears against the cold. Worker's clothes.

All the girls at the House would laugh to see her in such an outfit. "Are you sure you want me to wear this?"

"It'll keep attention off of you," he said. "Besides, I think it's cute."

"If you say so."

The outfit covered up her entire body, including every suggestion of a figure. She tied the sash around her waist, but the tunic still sagged around her.

"Context," Grau said, noticing her frown as she fussed with the fit. "Sure, it would be strange to wear that in the House of Perfumed Ribbons, but this is what common women wear while traveling all the time."

"You paid a lot just to get a common woman."

"I paid a lot for *you.* It doesn't matter what you're wearing. No one needs to know that underneath it all, those little ribbons are still hugging your thighs."

Her face burned.

And yet, something within her liked the idea of being a common woman on the outside, with her stockings a secret between them.

The landscape changed as they traveled that day. The

47

towns grew more infrequent and smaller. They stopped that night in a village that was hardly more than a cluster of cottages and a general store, with no inn. Grau rode through the dirty street until he found a house with horseshoes hanging in the windows. Grau said this was a symbol of hospitality.

"I stay with these people often when I'm coming home," he said. "I don't think we'll have any trouble here."

The woman at the door greeted him warmly but seemed surprised by Velsa. "Who is this?" she asked, but she was not unkind. Velsa immediately noticed the impact of her traveling clothes. Usually flesh and blood women treated her suspiciously or barely acknowledged her at all.

"My new traveling companion," Grau said. "Velsa."

"Not a concubine?" she asked. "I wouldn't take you for the type, Grau."

"The lonely type?" He looked wry. "You know how attached I am to Fern but she's not much of a conversationalist."

"Well, come in, both of you," the woman said. She put her hand atop Velsa's in greeting, which no woman had ever done before. Velsa almost drew back from sheer surprise. "I'm Morya. Make yourself at home. Horan, look at this—Grau has a concubine."

Horan squinted at them over an account book. He was a skinny man whose knobby hands and spectacles suggested that he occasionally paid for a little shape-shifting to his face to keep wrinkles away, but not much else. "A concubine? She's dressed like a stable boy."

"It's my fault," Grau said. "But find me a stable boy this pretty."

"That'll have to wait until morning," Horan joked. "And we charge extra for it, too."

Besides some initial surprise that Velsa could eat, her presence at the dinner table was accepted without much comment.

"Grau, aren't you supposed to join the border patrol?" Horan asked at dinner.

"Soon."

"I'd reconsider, if it's true about the dragon."

"Dragon?" Grau seemed close to laughter. "That's quite a rumor. A dragon, down here? If nothing else, the Miralem wouldn't put a precious dragon in danger. I heard there are only about fifty left in the whole world."

"I think there must be a few more than that," Horan said. "And I tell you, there's one in the mountains. Lots of people have seen it."

"Which people, dear?" the woman said, seeming as skeptical as Grau.

"Travelers!" Horan said. "The ones that come through all the time and talk to me for hours. Unlike you, I listen."

"Oh, what nonsense. If I don't listen, it's because I'm tired of tall tales. I'm sure if there was a dragon in the mountains we'd hear about it in the papers and not just in whispers."

"You don't think we'll ever really see a dragon, do you?" Velsa asked Grau that night as she settled into bed.

"No," he said, without hesitation, as he unbuttoned his boots. "They're very rare. They always have been, but loads of them died in the War of the Crystals. The population never recovered."

A fire-breathing dragon would have no trouble harming a Fanarlem.

"You're not afraid of a dragon, are you?" he asked.

"Shouldn't I be?"

"I'd like to see one," he said.

"A friendly one, maybe."

"From a comfortable distance," he agreed. "Of course. But they're the only magic beast left in the world."

"What happened to the rest?"

"They went extinct. People killed them. The dragons allowed themselves to be tamed in order to survive. They're clever enough to negotiate."

"That's sad, though."

He settled into bed beside her. "Kill or be killed. Control

49

or be controlled. You probably sympathize with the dragons now, don't you?"

"I do. But Fanarlem have no choice."

"I don't think the dragons really did either." She rested her head on the pillow, his head lifted just above her. She liked watching his face as he spoke; in the House she mostly only saw other Fanarlem faces. The girls didn't have quite so many subtleties of expression, so many small muscles. "Do you want me to set you free?" he asked.

"I'd be in far more danger if you set me free. I wouldn't know where to go."

His lips pressed together in a grim expression; when they parted again, his mouth had a faint wet sheen. For some reason it made her think of the flowers that bloomed outside the House in the spring, when the dew kissed them in the morning.

"I like having you with me," he said. "I didn't consider that you might resent anyone who owned you, doesn't matter who it is."

She was quiet, for a long moment, torn between all the things she had been taught and all the feelings buried deep within her. She wanted to be free, but she couldn't be free, and she hardly knew what it would mean. A simple path had been laid out for her, to share Grau's life as a willing servant and die with her soul redeemed. She imagined it would be a life of suffering, but this no longer felt true.

However, he seemed to question this path himself. It could only get them both in trouble.

Sometimes, all the eye could see were fields of brown grass, cut though with snaking streams, without a house to be seen. The roads had been built up above the fields, but they were mucky or washed out in sections and Grau led Fern very carefully.

This was the marshland.

"I grew up here," he told her. "It isn't to everyone's taste."

"I like it," she said.

"I thought you might. Mountains and beaches get all the

glory, but I always do my best thinking in the marshes."

In the late afternoon, a week since they had left Nisa, Grau looked at the landscape ahead. A solitary building poked distantly above the sea of grass.

"Hmm," he said, squinting. She had already come to realize that this was his favorite word. "That isn't right. Where is the house? This is the right place, I'm sure of it. Fern, where is the house?" Occasionally, he spoke to the horse. "I always stop with the Marnow family on my way home and all I see is the barn. I hope nothing happened…"

It was getting dark when they reached the barn, and the cold rain was starting up again. Grau was shivering even in his wool coat. The house was leveled, stones scattered throughout the marshes, leaving a foundation and the remains of furniture and broken plates.

"I can't believe it," he said. "I hope they're all right. They were such a nice family. At least we can still sleep in the barn."

"Grau, you're already cold! It'll be worse tonight." Thunder rumbled in the distance, and Velsa jumped.

"We get a lot of winter thunderstorms around here," he said, rubbing her back. "They come off Idle Lake in the north. We need shelter, even if it's shabby. Let's take a look inside."

He shoved open one of the large wooden doors with his shoulder. Within the barn were piles of hay that reached the rafters. The barn leaked in places, and some of the hay had molded. Grau sneezed.

"That's unfortunate," he said. "Still, we can create a little heat." He dug in his pocket and produced a crystal, not a mere light-stone, but a proper crystal, clear and multi-faceted.

"A crystal…" She marveled at it a moment. Crystals helped to capture and magnify magic, but they were certainly more expensive than anything the girls could afford.

"Magic can be done without crystals, as you saw when I grabbed that fire at the inn, but it is much more difficult. The crystal will help channel the elements. This hay spent plenty of time in the sun, and it still has the sun's power caught within it."

He pointed the crystal toward the piles of hay, sweeping it across in an arc, several times. He breathed deeply, in time with the rhythm.

He stopped to show her how the crystal was growing warmer. She put her fingertips to the smooth surface, which now felt like it had been resting near a fireplace.

"Now, we throw the magic back into the hay." He stepped forward forcefully, stomping the ground, and held the crystal outward. Steam rose from the hay in wisps, warming the air. He finished the magic with purposeful waves of his arms. The steam turned to clouds, so much that the room grew muggy.

Grau shrugged his coat off. "It won't last long," he said. "But it'll have to do. It won't be the nicest place we've ever slept, but we'll be home tomorrow and have our clothes washed."

She had some sympathy, now, for how the men who came to the House might not smell the best. It wasn't always easy to stay clean while traveling. Her fingers had a gray tinge, and Grau, admittedly, was looking pretty haggard with his hair and clothing wet.

He had just stepped out to bring in Fern when she heard a cough above her head. Followed by some male voices speaking in a confused whisper.

Velsa edged to the door.

Grau returned just as a man's face peered down from the loft. "Hey!" he shouted. "This is our damned barn. Find your own place to sleep!"

Behind him, another man said, "He warmed up the place. Maybe we should let him be."

"I'm not sleeping with a horse."

"Who are you?" Grau asked. "What happened to the Marnows?"

"None of your concern." The man climbed down the ladder, which Velsa hadn't even noticed until now, as it was in the shadows against the wall, and in fact, not so much as a ladder as a collection of hand-holds nailed into the planks. Velsa thought the object slung across his back was a rifle. She had never actually seen one, only heard the rumors of powerful new weapons.

"This land belongs to the Unified Army of the High Sorcerer," the man said, as soon as his boots hit the ground. He came marching up to them.

"I don't understand," Grau said.

"You don't need to understand anything more than that. This land belongs to Kalan Jherin now, and we're his representatives, so we'd appreciate if you move along."

Two more men were coming down the ladder. They all wore trim jackets styled unusually short, with hems that fell just a few inches below their belts. Their hair was also short, cut close around their ears. They must come from Nalim Ima, where the High Sorcerer Kalan Jherin kept his palace.

"We just want a place to spend the night," Grau said. "We'll move along in the morning. But I still want to know what happened to the Marnows. They wouldn't sell their land."

"Wouldn't they?" The men chuckled.

"I really don't think it would hurt if they spent the night," said the burliest of the men. He must have been six and a half feet tall. "Look at this girl he has with him."

"Where are the Marnows?" Grau demanded, clutching his crystal so they all could see it. "You expect me to believe that Kalan Jherin showed up, bought up their land and then leveled the house?"

The men all immediately shifted their rifles off their backs to point at Grau. "Put that away. We don't want any trouble," the third man said. Despite his reasonable words, he sounded a little drunk. "That's exactly what happened. The Marnows moved to the city."

Grau lowered his hand slightly. "Why would Kalan Jherin buy land out here?"

"To drain for farming. We're just guarding it now."

"Hey, lad," the burly man said. "Keep the barn heated and we'll let you stay."

Grau walked closer. "I've stayed with the Marnows when I come by here for the last five years. They would never sell their land without someone twisting their arm. And I'm no one's 'lad'. You're the ones who ought to move along. What is Kalan's army doing all the way out here anyway?"

The barrel of a rifle jabbed into Grau's stomach, forcing him to step back. "The High Sorcerer works for all Daramons," the first man said. "If I were you, I wouldn't question his decisions." Now he struck Grau in the side with the rifle.

"Sir!" The second man sounded disturbed. "I don't think we ought to be striking citizens."

"Bunch of bumpkins out here," the first man said. "No respect."

Grau glanced around with a wild spark in his eyes and spread his hands. The pile of hay exploded into a whirl of strands, obscuring her vision. The men coughed and choked, covering their faces against the assault of hay. The smell of mold must have been awful.

Grau swept an arm around her waist and pulled them both up onto Fern's back. He led the horse out the barn door and then spurred her to a gallop. Velsa was slung across Grau, her legs dangling over the side, but once they were moving he helped her into into her usual position.

Behind them, the three men emerged, shouting curses.

A shot whizzed through the rain, just past Grau. He leaned forward to lower his profile, holding her tight as if he needed to protect her, but he was in more danger than she was.

Another shot, and Fern reared back and let out a whinny of distress. Grau dug in, clutching the reins and Velsa tight. "Those bastards!"

No—no! Velsa couldn't bear that sweet Fern would be hurt…and worse might follow. The men were angry now and at least one of them had an eye on her. This could easily be the night when she was kidnapped, the night she lost the precious, fleeting life she had gained.

Fern, please. Please. She wrapped her arms around the horse's neck, such desperation pouring out of her that she felt hot and dizzy. A sensation washed over her, almost like hot water poured

54

over her head—or inside her head?

Somehow, Fern resumed her gallop.

Velsa kept her head bowed low. She didn't dare move, as if she had placed her own strength into Fern.

The distance between the horse and the three men grew wider. A few more shots fired, but they didn't reach. Fern's hooves pounded the path until they were safe enough—for now.

The sun was sinking below the horizon now, casting the sky in shades of pink and orange. It would soon be dark.

Grau slowed Fern to a walk. "We'd better stop a moment to see if Fern is hurt."

He dismounted and immediately had a look of consternation. "Here it is," he said. "Right in the ass! Poor girl. But she doesn't seem to be in pain anymore…" He opened his bag and got the healing balm for her wound.

He looked at Velsa.

"I—I don't understand," she said.

"Your telepathy," he said. "It breached the golden band. You were in such a panic that your power surged, so you could calm Fern and ease her pain."

"I couldn't," Velsa said, but hope fluttered in her chest. Power. He was saying she had power.

"You could." He spoke gravely, twisting the cap back on the healing balm. "You must not tell anyone this happened. People would be afraid of you."

"I saved us," Velsa said, lifting her fingers to the band.

"Yes, you did," he said. "Thank the fates for that. But a telepathic Fanarlem would still not be welcomed."

"The Halnari are welcomed," Velsa said. "They have telepathy."

But she already knew what he would say.

"They are loyal allies to Atlantis and Nalim Ima," Grau said. "Fanarlem aren't supposed to have power." He rubbed his forehead. "I'm sorry. We'd better keep moving. I don't know where else we could find shelter, so we'll have to keep going as long as we can."

CHAPTER FIVE

They reached Grau's home late the next day, after a miserable stretch of the journey. They had slept briefly in a shed for a few hours before sunrise, Grau shivering all night long although he was wrapped tight in blankets with her body in his arms. Rain had moved in not long after, and their clothes were sopping wet, penetrating her skin. If she was soaked through to the stuffing, she would be rendered almost immobile until she dried out. Luckily, it never went that far. Grau rushed them into the house and straight to the fireplace. It was already burning steadily, but he piled on a few more logs.

A woman hurried into the room to greet them. "Grau! I thought I heard you. Give me a hug."

"I'm soaked."

"I don't care. I haven't seen you in a month and when you go on patrol, well, what if I never see you again?"

"I'll be fine. Don't listen to those stories about the dragons."

"*Dragons?* I haven't even heard that. I'm talking about telepathic bandits. Now I have to worry about dragons, too?"

"Ma, this is Velsa."

"Welcome, Velsa!" she said, brushing off the dragons easily enough. "You are really…quite lovely. I was so worried this would be another time when Grau brings home something really bizarre."

He looked deeply embarrassed. "I've never brought any girl home before!"

"I was talking about that toad thing you had as a pet."

"You can't compare Velsa to a toad."

"Certainly I didn't mean that Velsa is a toad, but what I will say is simply that your standards of beauty are not always predictable."

"And besides, it wasn't a toad thing. It was just a toad. A blue-footed Atlantis marsh toad. They're very rare and the smartest member of the toad family." He looked at Velsa apologetically.

"I still don't really understand what the plan is," Grau's mother said. "I show the girl to your quarters, I suppose? It's a little awkward for me. I don't have a etiquette book on how to welcome a concubine. I remain skeptical as to whether this was a good idea."

"Of course it was a good idea," said a man now entering the room. "We went over this. Every boy wants to sow his oats on the road. It was safe back when I served, but do you want Grau falling into the clutches of some Miralem whore?"

"No, but, he's responsible for an actual person now."

"We aren't responsible for our servants? He's grown up. He can handle it. She's a Fanarlem. What is there to worry about? She doesn't eat. I'm sure she can also help him keep his things in order at camp and—can she cook?"

Grau waved his hand sideways. "Papa, can I talk to you a moment?"

"Anytime. Here, we'll step out away from the womenfolk."

They walked out onto the porch. Velsa could see the shape of them through the curtains. Grau was already gesturing a lot.

Grau's mother looked her over more closely. She had the same intent expression as her son. "I'm sorry about all this. You're not exactly what I expected. We have two Fanarlem who work for us, and…" She folded her hands into the sleeves of her robe. "Well, I never liked the idea. I don't think my son should buy a concubine. No offense."

58

"No offense taken. I don't have any choice in the matter," Velsa said.

"Garen feels this is preferable to leaving Grau to an unmarried life, but I don't know…" She snapped a look at the men on the porch. Then she leaned in closer. "Has he treated you well?"

"Yes, madam. Very well."

"Good. I would hope so." But now the older woman seemed at a loss in speaking to Velsa. "I suppose I might as well show you to his quarters."

She showed Velsa up the stairs. The house was substantial, about the same size as the House of Perfumed Ribbons. The furnishings didn't seem too grand, however, just normal wooden benches and tables. The plaster walls were painted with designs that had chipped with time. Rain made the rooms dim and Grau's mother didn't light any lamps or candles, so they certainly were not the wealthy people in novels who always had magical lights as bright as day in every room, but perhaps this was for the best. Velsa wasn't sure she would really want to live someplace ostentatious, undoubtedly with rules to match.

She sniffed the air. It had a damp, cold smell, almost like a cellar. Her clothes were still wet, since she had been led away from the fire, so once his mother left she took off her jacket and boots and climbed under Grau's blankets.

His desk was cluttered with bottles and bits of branches and leaves and pebbles, sprigs of dried herbs. A shelf held more of the same, plus some tools and small bottles. Evidence of half-finished projects; potion-making, perhaps. From the bed, she could see out the window to an endless sky.

I like him, she thought.

She couldn't imagine what his mother must think. What would she think, if she had a son who brought a concubine home?

But Velsa couldn't imagine having a son, or a husband, or any family at all. She had always lived in a strange world where family didn't exist, but everyone else in the House was the same sort of strange. Meeting Grau had brought her out of it, but he couldn't bring her into his world either. Grau could never think of marrying her even if he fell in love. She would always be an in-between person.

She heard his footsteps on the stairs and sat up, pushing off the covers. She didn't want him to think she'd been sleeping.

"I apologize," he said. "I had to explain to my father that you are more of a real girl than he anticipated."

Her nerves clenched. His father had truly been the one to suggest purchasing her. He must have certain expectations for her.

"I suppose it went as well as could be expected," Grau continued. "I told them I want you to be treated like any other guest. Let me find you something dry to wear for dinner."

He brought her a long tunic that belonged to his mother. She was swimming in it, but at least the cut was meant to be loose. She folded some of the excess fabric under the sash to keep the hem off the floor.

Grau had also changed, into a calf-length tunic of dark blue, with the skirts slit into four panels beneath the black sash belt. She had always found this to be a rather dashing style. Once, she had seen sword dancers on the street wearing them, the four panels twirling as they moved through the forms.

A few candles lit the long table, with a spread of rice with smoked fish, stewed vegetables and dark green salad. Now another young man was here, bearing a strong resemblance to Grau—one of the brothers, obviously. A young woman was rushing to the table as well. She was nearly as tall as Grau, and wore a shirt and trousers, which didn't quite seem to meet with parental approval judging by the frowns of Grau's father and mother. Her hair was in a coiled braid like a crown around her head, but strands had broken free.

"You're late," the brother said. "So time consuming to put on clean trousers for dinner."

"Oh, hush." She plopped into a chair and reached for the wine.

"Velsa, this is my little sister Preya," Grau said. "And my older brother Agrin. He's the only one still at home, but not for long."

"You got the latest circulations in town, didn't you, Grau?" asked Grau's father.

"Yes—they're still in my bag. Should I fetch them?"

"Velsa could get them," Grau's father said.

"No, I want her to just relax," Grau said. "And I'm the one who knows where I put them."

"I spent two hundred and twenty ilan on her, so I hope you're planning on having her do something!"

"I'll be right back," Grau said irritably. He rushed up the stairs.

His mother gave Velsa a gentle look and then said, "Garen, I know the whole thing was your idea, but I think you'd better stay out of it."

"It's a lot of money," he muttered, spooning sauce onto his rice. He glanced at Velsa when he put the bowl of vegetables aside, and then craned his neck closer. "What's around your neck? That isn't a golden band, is it?"

The rest of Grau's family also looked at her now.

She drew her hands into her lap. This was the first time in days her clothing had even put the band on display. "It is, sir, but —I don't have any telepathy. I've always had this and it blocks my abilities." Of course, if she really had calmed Fern, this was no longer entirely true.

"What in the seven curses… *Grau!*"

Grau came back with an arm full of bound pamphlets. This had been one of his last stops in town.

"She's telepathic?" his father cried.

"No. I mean, not really, it's under control. She has a golden band."

"But of all the concubines to choose…"

Agrin seemed amused. He said, "Pa, she has a golden band and papers. What else is Grau supposed to say? Maybe she was the best looking girl they had."

61

"Don't they all look the same?" Grau's father said. "I worry that the time may come when Grau could get in trouble just for having a telepath with him, bands and papers aside. If we go to war, and everyone's on edge…"

"She isn't a Miralem," Grau said. "She's a Fanarlem. She might become *valuable*. And the Halnari are Miralem too, but they're our allies. No one seems to mind that they have telepathy."

"I think Grau's right," his mother said. "Lord Jherin always wants loyal telepaths. He pays good money for them. Not that it matters when she has a band."

"Hrmph." His father opened a pamphlet to read over his plate. "Maybe. It all makes me nervous until I know which way the wind is blowing."

Grau's mother and siblings reached for the rest of the pamphlets. Pages opened all around the table.

"It makes *me* nervous to send Grau to the border with all this tension," his mother murmured. "Lord Jherin promises so much, but it's nothing to him if some boys out in the wilderness get sent to the slaughter…"

"It's just a patrol," Grau's father said. "Don't think too much of a few stories. You have to remember how many miles the border goes on for, and most of the trouble comes from bandits and nomads."

"Grau said there were dragons!"

"I said there *weren't* dragons," Grau said. "Because it's true. That's completely absurd."

"Assumptions like that are how people get killed," his mother said firmly.

"This reminds me," Grau said. "Do you know what happened to the Marnow farm, exactly?"

"Tornado," Agrin said.

"A real tornado?" Grau asked. "Or a magic one?"

"Well, it's a funny thing about the Marnows," his father said. "A few months back, I heard, some men came up the river from Atlantis and asked to buy their land and they said no. Then this tornado hits, and now they've decided to say yes."

"So that's how it is." Grau gripped his fork. "I knew they wouldn't sell willingly. I came across some very ill-mannered soldiers in the barn."

"Don't worry, the powers that be won't come this far," his father said. "Yet, anyway."

"Still..." Grau poked his salad. His mother briefly stood and filled his glass with wine.

"The marsh goes on and on," she said. "There will still be plenty left."

Velsa glanced at Grau with understanding. If there was a place in the world that belonged to her, she would love it too—every inch of it.

"Hey, Preya," said Agrin. "Lord Jherin is recruiting women now."

"For what?" she scoffed. "Having babies?"

"No. Well, maybe, but it says 'A variety of roles'."

"Let me see that." She grabbed the pamphlet.

"*You* are definitely not going to work for Kalan Jherin," her father said, with the air of a final word. "Your husband is already waiting."

"My 'husband' doesn't care if I live or die as long as I pop some babies out of my loins."

"Stars above, Preya, have a little dignity," her mother said. "He doesn't know you yet. It's always the way."

"I don't care if he lives or dies either."

"He's a very nice young man and the Hohrlens are such a good family. I know you're excited to live in Atlantis. Aren't you?"

"I'd like to see Atlantis," she said, stabbing a carrot. "But not under these circumstances."

Grau's mother sighed. "Can we at least try to act the part of a well-bred family at dinner?"

After dinner, Grau and his family were still discussing politics and war. Velsa didn't know much about it. Politics did not affect the House. Even if the men went away to fight, soldiers would always have to travel up and down the Atlantis River, and they would always stop in Nisa, and they would always seek out girls. The only way war would change their lives would be if the Miralem fought their way south and conquered the city. Miralem didn't believe in Fanarlem slavery, and all the girls would be turned out. Inevitably, most of them would have turned to prostitution, which Miralem did not ban.

Grau said, "You could sit by the fire in the parlor, if you like. Plenty of books to read."

"We could play chatrang," Preya suggested. Her golden eyes—even more catlike than Grau's—were bright, but her tone was almost shy.

"Okay." Velsa didn't know the game, but she was so surprised that Grau's sister was willing to offer friendship to a concubine.

Preya put a few fresh logs on the parlor fire and set up a game-board. It was a square grid. Each player had two rows of black and white pieces in little carved shapes such as kings, soldiers, and horses. She explained the rules rather half-heartedly.

"It's a well-mannered thing to do while you have a conversation," she said with a shrug. "Unless you want to be like my brothers and get very competitive about it, and have a huge fight about whether you took your hand off of a piece or not, and throw the board off the table."

"I don't think I want to do that," Velsa said.

"Wise choice," Preya said. "It'll be nice to have another girl around. I see my brother's wives fairly often but they're very... wife-y."

"I take it you're not looking forward to being a wife?"

"To say the least," Preya said. "The future seems more unbearable the closer it gets. Parties and dances and babies? I have no interest in any of that. I mean, babies are cute, but that only goes so far."

"What is it that you like to do?" Velsa asked.

"I'd join the military if I could. Like Grau. Or maybe even

the navy. I've heard that they're building spectacular new ships in Nalim Ima, powered by steam. I know the seafaring life isn't as romantic as it sounds, but I can't help imagining. As it stands, I agreed to the marriage because at least it would get me out of this backwater."

"Grau seems to miss the backwater."

"But, you notice, he doesn't stay."

They traded a few moves as they spoke. Velsa thought the game was actually quite interesting, the way each piece had different ways of navigating the board. There was a lot of thinking to be done. Preya obviously had no interest in actually playing the game, though. "You're really very pretty," she said.

"We're made to be admired," Velsa said. "But I have nothing to do with it."

"All the Fanarlem around here are kind of scary to look at."

"Are there many Fanarlem around?" Velsa had seen very few Fanarlem since she left the House. Occasionally, they might pass a laborer or a servant girl on the street.

"We have two house servants and a few more working the farm," Preya said. "They almost never speak but they'll *stare* at you. When Papa said Grau was going to buy a Fanarlem girl I thought they were crazy. But now I see." She moved a piece into a pretty bad position. "I suppose you've probably had an exciting life."

"Not at all," Velsa said. "I grew up in one building and we rarely left."

"Oh. I imagined those Perfume Houses…the better ones, anyway…were a decadent party every night, with famous people stopping in, and music and wine…"

Velsa shook her head. "I was only in the House proper for two weeks, anyway. The mistresses of the house are nice, but they're eager to get rid of us. I suppose eighteen years is a long time to sit on investments."

"If you're created specifically to be a concubine," Preya said, "then how do they know, when they create you, that you're

65

really a girl?"

"They don't," Velsa said. "They have some tests, but sometimes they get it wrong. There was a girl in my year like that. She started out in the house of male concubines, but she acted like a girl, and said she was a girl, and talked like a girl, so they moved her into our House. Male concubines aren't worth quite as much, so they get upset when it goes the other way, but there's no use trying to sell a girl if she won't act like one."

"Did Grau tell you about me?"

"No…"

"I'm attracted to women. Not men." Preya was blunt, but she said it like she was confessing a curse. Velsa supposed she was, considering how much flesh and blood people spoke of marriages and heirs.

"I've heard there is a house for Fanarlem girls who favor other girls, and Fanarlem men who favor other men," Velsa said. "Maybe your husband would let you have a concubine."

"But I still have to sleep with *him*. Besides, he'd hate that idea. He's very traditional." Preya looked sly. "Who would have guessed I'd be jealous of Grau's concubine?"

Velsa felt a twinge of embarrassment, but then, Preya's flirtation seemed so different than any man, even Grau. And she looked so very much *like* Grau.

"It is strange," Velsa said. "No one ever asked me if I liked men or women. And really, they made it sound like we *would* be afraid of men and find them unpleasant."

"Was it all right…with Grau?"

Velsa fumbled with her game piece, realizing she had steered the conversation in a bad direction. She had no idea Daramon women were so interested to ask about these things.

When Velsa didn't answer immediately, Preya said, "He better not have hurt you!"

"No, no. We haven't even…"

"Oh. *Really?*" Preya hissed. "Stars! You're getting better treatment than I will when I marry *Morilan Hohren*." Her tone was scathing. Velsa couldn't imagine what the wedding might be like.

Preya didn't seem like the type of girl who could pretend to be something she wasn't, not even for a night. "And Grau must be completely mad about you. Magic has always fascinated him."

"I hope I'm more than just an interesting *spell*," Velsa said.

"Of course. I always say the wrong thing," Preya said. "I just mean that I think any girl Grau spent time with would need some magic in her blood, because that's what interests him. He's not very good with parties and dances, and he gets bored easily, and once he decides he doesn't like something, he's over the entire experience and everyone involved."

Velsa had never noticed Grau getting bored. In fact, he seemed interested in everything, but she realized in their short time together, every day was a new place with new people. "I hope he doesn't get bored with me…"

"I mean, like card parties. Frivolous stuff. We're just stubborn. Grau and I have always been close, you know, being the youngest and the strangest members of the family."

Velsa finally stopped trying to think about the board. "Your parents are really going to marry you to a man when you like other women?"

"Yes. I told Mama. I haven't ever said anything to Papa, and I won't dare, but it wouldn't matter. Mama said I need to master my feelings."

"I never realized flesh and blood women had so little freedom either…" Velsa's understanding of the lives of real women had, until now, been confined to novels. Some of the women in novels had arranged marriages, but they always seemed delighted by them. Of course, the House library would not have been stocked with novels about women who defied their fate and behaved willfully.

"My brothers' wives seem happy," Preya said. "I just can never be happy marrying a man, especially Morilan. Still, at least he won't own me…though I'm sure Grau will never treat you poorly." Velsa saw denial in Preya's eyes, as if she could not quite accept that her brother owned another person. But she didn't seem to have any such qualms about the family's Fanarlem servants. Because Velsa was beautiful and educated, they could forget that she had the same damaged soul as every other Fanarlem.

"When are you supposed to marry Morilan Hohren?" Velsa asked.

Preya laughed. "Isn't his name alone just awful? Oh, I have some months yet. I'm trying to think of another plan. I do wonder about the Kalanites recruiting women...but I'm not sure I trust Kalan Jherin. He's the one who started all of this. It wasn't so shameful to be a lesbian a century ago, but he promoted marriage and large families during the War of Crystals."

"Everyone talks about Kalan Jherin," Velsa said. "I thought he was the leader of Nalim Ima, not our country."

"Kalan Jherin isn't the leader of Nalim Ima either," Preya said. "Not exactly. He's the *Wodrenarune*, the most powerful sorcerer in all the known world, and the fates have chosen him to guide us. All the leaders listen to him, in Atlantis and throughout the islands, in Nalim Ima and New Sajinay... Nalim Ima is simply where he lives."

"What is he guiding us to? Standing against the Miralem?"

"Yes, and one must admit he's done a good job of it. I never know what to think, because Miralem women have so much more freedom and they can love whomever they want, but just the thought that they can get in your head with telepathy..." She shuddered. "And they think they're better than us. It must be nice enough to be a Miralem woman, but it wouldn't be nice at all to be a Daramon woman in a Miralem world. I can't win."

Velsa kept talking to Preya for hours, eventually winning the game to Preya's indifference, while Grau spent time with his parents and brother. When they were still talking well past dark, Preya offered to style Velsa's hair.

"Hair is my favorite right now," she said. "I just bought a pamphlet showing all the latest styles."

"If you're gentle," Velsa said, protective of her hair. "It doesn't grow back. I need to wash it, at some point..." Velsa gently brushed all the dirt and dust out of her hair every morning, but over time it tended to look a little flat, especially lately with all their traveling and sleeping closer to Grau.

"I could wash it too! I'll be oh-so-gentle," Preya promised.

Velsa was happy to pass this task onto someone else. Her hands were waterproof, but not her arms, and handling water made her nervous. Preya heated some water and brought a pitcher upstairs to her room, and had Velsa lean back over a washstand. She was very careful, working soap and water up Velsa's hair from the ends to her scalp so her face didn't get a drop on it. Her touch was soothing, almost sensual.

Velsa thought again of Preya's blunt admission that she liked women rather than men. This was still the difference between a girl like Preya and a girl like Velsa. Preya had enough freedom to realize what she liked, even if she couldn't have it.

Velsa didn't dare consider what she liked, beyond Grau.

However, this was also the first time she had been away from him for any stretch since he acquired her, and she missed him by the time he came to bed late. She had already been sleeping.

They woke late, well rested. Grau sprung out of bed and parted the curtains. "Perfect...the rain is over. We can go out roaming." Her clothes were pressed and folded neatly, as if by magic, but likely by invisible servants. Fanarlem servants, perhaps. She wondered what they thought, pressing the clothes of a Fanarlem girl.

Best not to think of that and cloud the day. She slid out of the covers, drowsily tugging on her pants. Grau wore a long belted coat, boots and hat, quite similar to her own outfit, and was entirely dressed before she'd placed a foot on the floor. He fetched some food from the kitchens and soon they were stepping outside, to the chill mist and beautiful rosy light of morning.

The sky today was mostly blue, and she had a better look at the stone house and barn, which stood alone with fields of grasses in every direction. Here and there rose forests of bushes, with long-necked water birds perched on the branches.

Occasionally a lone tree stood, and farther in the distance still, soft hills swathed in low clouds. Out here, it seemed hard to believe the city even existed. Surely the grasses must go on forever.

Wind whipped gently at their clothing. Grau led the way down a path cut through the grass.

"I can't believe the Marnow land is sold," he said. "And there's nothing I can do."

"How much does land cost out here?" she asked.

"I don't know, but certainly more than I have, and what does it matter if Kalan's army is willing to use any means necessary?" He thrust his hands in his pockets. "Reading the pamphlets last night, I saw that Kalan Jherin is also looking for sorcerers. It's awfully tempting to try and go there, when my patrol stint is over. They say Kalan Jherin rewards his magic users very well."

"Would you want to work for him? Considering all this?"

"I don't really know if Lord Jherin is aware of what goes on all the way out here," Grau said. "This must be a pretty unfavorable posting. I hear it's very different in Nalim Ima. Even more cosmopolitan than Atlantis. I'd have the chance to work with some of the best sorcerers in the world, without paying for schooling, and if I manage to impress some higher-ups, perhaps I could assure the safety of this land."

"In that case, why wouldn't you do it?"

"Because any spells I develop would belong to him. I couldn't take credit for them, and I couldn't sell the instructions. Of course, spells are always pirated, so it isn't as if I'd lose much money there, but...I *do* want credit." He scuffed his boot through the dirt. "I suppose if I was a good citizen, I wouldn't care."

"Why wouldn't he allow you to take credit for your work?" As she spoke, her eyes scanned the path. The grass all looked the same at a glance, but up close she noticed the monotone sea of brush was actually comprised of many different plants. Mixed in with the light brown grass were shrubs with tiny red leaves, and thorny plants with little black berries. She gathered a few different seed pods into her hands as they passed.

"I'm sure they'd say it undermines the unity of Kalan's followers. Promotes jealousy. But I can't like it. In business, you have to be a little bit competitive."

She smiled a little. "I'm learning a lot about you here."

"Oh? What did Preya tell you?"

"She said you get bored easily."

"Well—"

"But you won't get bored of me. That's what she claimed." She had never teased him before. It might've been a risk, but honest words slipped out so easily here.

"As Preya goes, I suppose that was pretty restrained. But I'm sure I won't get bored of you. I knew from the first moment, something about you would suit me, that you'd like the marshes…" He stopped and took her hand, the one that clasped the seed pods.

For a moment she thought he might kiss her.

She wasn't sure why she would think that. Men didn't usually want to kiss the dry mouths of their Fanarlem concubines.

He was just looking at the seed pods. "You can use these for protection spells," he said. "I like to brew them with the bark of the eagle trees, like that one in the distance. They make your skin more resistant."

She half-smiled. She was thinking of kisses and he was thinking of brewing spells out of bark. She realized she was constantly preparing herself for the moment when he would drop this preamble and transform into the man she had always expected to have as her master, the one who saw her as a strictly sexual being.

Would he wait for weeks, months? Years? Until she made the first move?

She wondered what he would do if she kissed him. But no one had trained her for that.

"What would you think about going to Nalim Ima?" he asked.

"I don't know much about it. I don't think we had any

71

customers from there. It's pretty far away, isn't it?"

"Yes. It's a large island across the sea."

"What do they…think of Fanarlem concubines there?"

"I really don't know. It would be an adventure, and if it was really terrible I guess we could come home. I can always sell fish if I have to."

He came to a spot where the path curved and sloped downward. It was really less of a path and more of a puddle by now, after the rains.

"We're almost there," he said, pointing ahead to a canoe that was parked in the muddy ground up the bank of a stream.

Grau paced around the canoe for a moment, like he was looking for something. Then he stepped back. He jerked his hands up and the standing water in the body of the canoe flooded out, down the sides. She jumped with surprise.

"How far do your powers extend, anyway?" she asked. "You did that without even needing the crystal!"

"This is home. I know all the energies of the land. It looks easy, but it took months of practice as a kid." He wiped the seats of the canoe with the edge of his coat and motioned for her to climb in.

"This is the fun part." He grinned and lifted his hands. The mud began to slide, and the canoe with it, dropping them in the water with a jolt and a splash.

She laughed. She couldn't remember the last time she'd really laughed, with abandon.

He smiled back at her, his eyes squinted against the sun, as he lifted up the paddle and pushed off into the stream.

The canoe slid past the brown grasses, down the gently winding waters. She heard rustling in the grass, and saw ripples from small creatures. It was so tranquil here that she really could see forgetting her past before long.

"Do you want to try a little sorcery?" he asked. "Chances are, you won't be able to do it on your first try, but one must start somewhere." He put the warm crystal in her hand. "See if you can feel the threads of magic around us."

72

She eagerly cupped the crystal between her hands, now hearing the whispering of the grass in the wind almost as if it were a language. The water had a healing glow, an aura of shimmering green. She felt the slithering of a nearby water snake before she saw it, and turned to see the black curve of its tail disappear out of sight. And she felt it within her own body, too. She was made of forest and field. Just as it was clear when a tree or a meadow was alive even though it didn't breathe, she understood now how Grau felt her own life, even as she slept. All her senses were heightened, and undiscovered senses threatened to emerge.

"Do you feel that?" he asked.

"Yes. Everything is so much more...*more.*"

"Someday, I'll have to get you a crystal of your own," he said. "You take to it well."

"I haven't done any magic yet."

"You feel things right away. I didn't have that luck trying to teach Preya. She can't still her mind long enough to listen."

"Why is it that sorcery is all right, but telepathy is so frightening?"

"Daramons are dependent on the resources around them. I can do elemental magic when there are elements around, but if not, I have to create or buy spells and carry them with me. Miralem can do telepathy anywhere, and from great distances. And besides, talented telepaths can read minds, manipulate minds, even rip the soul from the body. The only reason Daramons have gained any ground at all is because of the Ten Thousand Man Sacrifice."

"Why do I have telepathy, then?"

"You must have been a Miralem, in your past existence." He grinned. "The enemy."

"Will the time ever come...when you could take off my band?"

He shoved the canoe away from the grasses where it was drifting to a stop, and kept it paddling toward the autumn-bare branches of the bushes that hung over the water. "Sometimes untrained telepaths don't have the best control, and if you used your power in a fit of emotion—it could be very bad."

"My emotions are pretty controlled."

He poked the paddle through the water. Pretending to paddle, more so than paddling.

"If the time comes that I deem it safe, I will certainly take off the band," he said, a firm edge entering his tone. "But it doesn't feel safe now."

She nodded faintly.

He put a hand on her knee. "I trust *you*, the time just isn't right. I certainly wouldn't mind having a telepath on my side. A telepath and a sorcerer together can accomplish nearly anything. It's how you were made, after all, with both kinds of magic."

"Was I?" He was right. She didn't know much about the world, not even exactly how Fanarlem were created.

"Each little piece of you needs its own spell. A spell so your skin can feel, a spell so your bones will move, a spell that gives strength to your stuffing so you can lift and clench things. At the end, the sorcerer will weave you with illusions so you look just the right amount of real. But that's just your body, and the body is nothing without a soul. At the end, a telepath must call your soul into your eyes and give them life."

"It sounds very complicated," she said.

"It is. Often, several different sorcerers must make the spells. I'll bet their initials are carved onto you somewhere."

She supposed to a sorcerer, a Fanarlem was an apex demonstration of magic.

"Did they give you different bodies to grow into?" he asked.

"Yes. They give us three before the final one, which we get at fourteen." A Fanarlem's soul rested in their eyes, so when her body was changed as she grew, only the eyes had to be moved. The child bodies were then reused on other girls, but their faces were always individual.

"It must be jarring."

"I'm always very clumsy for a few weeks. But I like getting

taller."

"I like getting taller too. Lots of pressure on Daramon men to be tall."

"You're quite tall."

"But I don't know what boy doesn't worry about it, growing up. If you end up short, the teasing is merciless. You can go to a Halnari shape-shifter in the city and get them to add a couple inches if you can afford it. One of my friends did and it made him clumsy at first, too. And achy, for days. It's hard to shape-shift *well*."

"There are a lot of expectations on all of you, aren't there?" Velsa asked.

"Did Preya tell you about her situation?"

"Yes."

"I think maybe she *should* go work for Kalan Jherin," he said. "My parents might despair, but that marriage will bring her despair tenfold."

"Could we all go together?"

"Maybe. But I have to finish my time on patrol. I'd be back just in time to save Preya from her wedding."

CHAPTER SIX

Slowly, hour by hour and day by day, Velsa began to enjoy the moments of her life. Preya gossiped about her friends in town and taught Velsa a dance. Sometimes Velsa was left alone to read their books, which held much more variety than the educational volumes in the House library. Grau took her riding to the top of a hill for a picnic, and on another day they went on a quest for a blue-footed Atlantis marsh toad. He said they mostly lived on the island in the middle of the lake. They rode in the canoe to the lake where his family raised the fish that had secured their fortunes, and then spent the day roaming the island.

When he triumphantly placed in her palm a small, fat toad with eyes that squinted calmly, she thought it was the most beautiful gift anyone could give her.

"What makes it the smartest member of the toad family?" she asked.

"Oh—I read that in a book, but I'm not sure. I haven't, personally, been able to coax any great displays of intelligence from a toad. But it's cute, isn't it?"

"Not a bad first girlfriend," she said. "I'm not sure what your mother was complaining about."

Of course, they let the toad go. It surely would not be as happy held captive.

Grau's father was gone most of the day working in town, so she only saw him in the evening. He was the only thing she feared. If someone needed wine at the dinner table, he would ask her to pour. When he noticed Grau rubbing his shoulder as if it ached he said, "Why don't you have your girl do that?" It was plain that Grau's father didn't think Velsa should be treated as a member of the family.

One night, she had come to bed a little before Grau once again, when she heard his father stop him in the hall.

"Why did I pay two hundred and twenty ilan for that girl?" he asked bluntly.

"What do you mean?"

"She isn't doing her duty."

"I don't know what you're talking about."

"Oh, come on, Grau. You are not having her for her intended purpose."

"I'll decide what her purpose is."

"You're besotted with her, aren't you? It happens, I suppose, but remember, she's a Fanarlem. It benefits her to be kept in her place. Every time you bed her, you're helping her learn humility and submission."

"I would hope she doesn't feel *humility* when I bed her."

"But she should. When she dies, the fates will look kindly on her. You don't have to feel guilty about enjoying her. Don't forget what she is and that she belongs to you."

"She'll hear you," Grau hissed.

"I hope she does. But in the end, you're the one who needs to draw the line."

A moment later, Grau opened the door. He looked at her, his eyes like storms.

She sat up in bed, her tiredness brushed aside. One strap of her chemise fell off her shoulder and she didn't bother to lift it.

"I heard him," she said.

He shook his head. "My father doesn't understand. It's not his place to tell us when we should..."

"But I...I'm scared he might send me away." She tried to scramble out from under the covers, but her movements were jerky. She was scared—and yet, not just scared.

She *did* like him. Something in his eyes had compelled her from the first moment they met, the same as he had clearly felt toward her. And some part of her wanted to surrender fully to that feeling. "I think...I might not mind," she said. "I think I might like it."

He crossed the room to sit on the bed beside her. "For weeks I have slept so close to you. Dreaming of the day you would be fully mine...but...I don't want it to be because my father said so."

"Maybe the time is right." She had already been so close to him, but this still seemed very different. She wondered how it would feel, if it would hurt—or maybe it would be the best feeling of her life, to have his hands and body engage her as deeply as his eyes already did.

He reached for her face. His fingers stroked her cheek, briefly. "Velsa...I don't want to *take* you. I want to *bring* you happiness. I want to make love to you."

She shivered.

He pushed the covers fully off of her and crawled toward the corner where the bed met the wall, where she always slept. He kissed her forehead, and then her cheekbone, and then her mouth.

She blinked at him. He was kissing her, and it was such a tender gesture, just like she imagined. His eyes regarded her softly in the candlelight, golden light flickering on his left cheek, while the other half of his face lay in shadow.

"It's true," he said. "I'm falling in love with you. I think maybe I was in love with you from the start, or at least from the minute I saw that your only possession was a box of rocks...but I want you too. I don't know, sometimes, if I'm a brute lusting for your beauty and the strange magic you're made of, or if I'm... your friend. Your friend who loves to talk to you and to know what you're thinking."

Your friend... Why did that bring a lump of pain to her throat, of all the words?

She stroked his hair. He had bathed earlier; his hair was still a little wet at the ends, soft and black.

Her innards felt like they were buzzing.

She moved her hand down, to his cheek, to stroke the edge of his chin. He had shaved, but still, his skin was a little rough, while hers was soft as velvet.

What if she loved him back? Truly loved him?

She stood on a precipice. If she dared to fall, then— That was when he really would have the power to hurt her.

But I already like him.

Maybe she had fallen without knowing it, almost from the start. She crushed her lower lip beneath her teeth, causing brief jabs of pain.

"What *are* you thinking, Velsa? I never really know."

She couldn't find the words to explain the depth of her fear. It was no use. Right now he believed he would love her forever, and he never seemed to understand what it was like to be her, to have her life in his hands at every moment.

But she wanted him. She couldn't really be sure if she wanted him because she wanted him, or if she just couldn't bear the tension of his desire anymore.

Maybe it was both.

Yes. Certainly, it was both, and they tangled together. She wanted him to desire her. He was the only man she had ever met who made her feel that way.

Her actions would speak louder than words. She put her hands to the button just below his collar and unfastened it, revealing a triangle of his skin. Her hands worked their way down until his shirt was open. She trailed her fingertips along the lean muscle of his chest, feeling the slow rise and fall of his breath. He was so solid, so complicated with his real flesh and bone and blood flowing through veins. She felt like a breath of air, hardly real at all, just skin and bones and fluff.

And a damaged soul inside.

She remembered him saying, *What if it wasn't true, and you felt bad for no reason?*

He shrugged his shirt off, with the faintest smile like he

feared this might scare her. Then he pushed the other strap of her chemise off her shoulder, and peeled the bodice down to reveal her small breasts. Her torso was stitched at the sides with thread the same color as her skin, so her chest and stomach were unmarred by any seams, just the indent of a navel like any real girl. In the candlelight her skin looked golden.

"The sight of you is worth waiting for," he said.

She used to wonder, sometimes, if men ever got a Fanarlem girl home and changed his mind when he saw the reality of her artificial form. Her body seemed a shameful thing, the charade of a real woman, and what beauty she had did not feel like her own but rather something that was placed upon her. She grew up knowing that the man who bought her might want to change her. He might decide she needed larger breasts or the exotic touch of red hair—more expensive features that would always be added after purchase.

It was so different now, far from the House, seeing herself in Grau's eyes. To him, she was a work of craftsmanship. She couldn't take credit for that, but it made her wonder if the person who made her thought of his work the way Grau thought of his magic.

Whatever the case, this body was hers now. She could settle into this skin because he obviously didn't want to change it.

He continued to pull the undergarment down, tossing it aside, leaving her naked except for the stockings.

He lay down beside her, putting his arms around her, gathering her close, skin to skin. His warmth seemed to slowly melt into her, and as always it felt like something she remembered, being warm from within.

He nudged her hair away from her neck, placing kisses there that barely brushed her skin. She felt her body relax, her legs parting, her back melting into the pillows, like a flower opening to the spring. He ran his hands along her thighs, pausing when he found the little buttons sewn to the back of her legs that were hidden beneath the ribbons. He unbuttoned them, and loosened the ribbons, and slowly peeled the silk away from her skin, as he kept kissing her neck and chest and finally, her breasts.

She had always expected, when the moment came, to feel like a slave submitting to her duty, so it was surprising how much this seemed the opposite. His soft kisses made her feel like something so treasured that it was she who had his heart—she who could hurt him. He ran a hand over her breast, her stomach, her thigh, and she looked at him through her long lashes, making no move to touch him in return, although he was also beautiful, with his lean, strong body, his olive skin, his light brown eyes slightly slanted and mysterious. The pulse of life within him that stirred her soul as if she hadn't really lived until she felt the beat of his heart.

"Velsa…" He suddenly gathered her up in his arms, holding her against him and under him, not quite placing his full weight upon her. His erection pressed against her and he let out a shuddering breath into her ear.

"Go slowly," she whispered.

He climbed out of bed, cold air rushing in behind him. She propped herself up on one elbow, watching him rummage in his bag. He took out the small bottle of oil that Dalarsha must have given him.

"Let's try this…" He poured a little onto his fingers. "Letting it warm up a bit…"

He slid his fingers inside her, swirling the warm oil to coat the surface of her passage, and an unexpected tremble of pleasure made her gasp.

"Oh—oh dear," she said. "This feeling…"

"Does it hurt?" His movements stopped.

"No…," she groaned.

"Have you never pleasured yourself?"

"No…no. I didn't even have those parts until my final body, and they told us that if we touched them, they'd strip our hands off. We're supposed to be pure until the day we're acquired…"

"Well, that doesn't help anything. I don't approve." His two fingers now slowly stroked along the top side of her passage, and his thumb reached up to stroke the little fold between her mounds, so his fingers seemed to pinch her in a vise of pleasure. Ripples of sensation fluttered through her.

"Although maybe there is something to it," he said, "because you look so deliciously surprised..."

Her back arched. She stared at the ceiling, clawing the sheet. Her legs were utterly limp but her toes curled. Her entire body seemed to be narrowing to a pinpoint and was the heat inside her only her imagination?

"Grau..."

He sped up the motion of his thumb. She felt like there was a bird beating its wings inside her, begging to be set free. She gasped for breath, feeling like she needed to draw in air for the first time in her life.

He drew his hand away.

"No, no, please don't stop," she begged.

"Let me be inside you when you release, bellora..."

'Bellora' was a word that unmarried men in the land called eligible women of their class, but for married men, this term of endearment was only for their wives. She wondered which way he meant it, but either way, no Fanarlem girl was called 'bellora'.

She could hardly bear the moments it took him to remove his pants and resettle beside her. He drew the blanket over them, sheltering them against the cold room. He pressed her shoulders against the wall beside the bed, pinning her in a nest of warmth.

He gazed at her, drawing out the moment, to her exquisite torture. His hands grazed her thighs and stomach, coming just short of touching her between the legs again.

"Are you sure you're ready for this?" he asked impishly.

"Grau, *please.*"

He wrapped his hands around her buttocks and slowly pierced her. She dug her fingernails into his back.

"Does it hurt?"

"A little, but..."

"That is a tight little space," he said. "Of course, I'm sure they have this all planned out at the House of Perfumed Ribbons.

It certainly wouldn't be good for business if any man had to order a *smaller* part. If it keeps hurting, we could maybe… customize you a little better."

"You talk too much," she said, her body still hungry for what his hand had promised.

"Yes, madam."

He thrust deeper, still gripping her bottom, and then slowly drew out—almost all the way—then slowly slid his way back in. He filled her completely, and she almost felt like he could tear her up, but the pain seemed to ebb after a few strokes. She grabbed his hair, maybe a little too hard, as if some part of her wanted to cause him pain too. He drew in a sharp breath but didn't fight her.

"Oh, Velsa…I'm so glad you're mine…" He kissed her fully now, his tongue in her willing mouth. She tasted mint—it had seasoned their salad at dinner. His weight pressed upon her fully, her rib cage creaking with protest, but she was made of strong enough stuff for this, and she didn't have to breathe. She liked the feeling of him crushing her, his hips rocking deep into her—she felt like she was becoming a part of him. His fingers entwined with hers. He held her hands against the mattress.

I will belong to this man forever, she thought. It was a fact, but just now it was also a comfort. She felt safe, and deeply valued. Her skin was alive with his touch, sensations rolling through her core.

If only life could always be this simple.

His motions quickened. She moaned. Her body hovered on the brink of explosion. She shifted the angle of her hips, trying to get to the spot that never seemed to quite be fulfilled. She drew her knees up higher, wrapping her legs around him.

Something was happening, warmth and a pleasure that was almost pain, and yet not pain at all. She cried out, and then clamped her mouth shut because she didn't want his family to hear—even if it would shut his father up. Waves of joy shuddered down her legs; just when she feared it might end there was another.

83

As it was finally ebbing, he suddenly sped up and she cried out again. It was too much now; she was so tender. He gripped her tightly and she felt his hot seed inside her. She didn't move at first; she wanted to feel it before the vanishing spell swallowed it up. He slowed, shuddering, gently kissing her cheek as his own climax came to an end.

He drew out of her carefully.

She stared at the ceiling with wonder. He was breathing hard, and almost laughed. "That was all right, wasn't it?"

"Yes…," she murmured dreamily.

He picked up one of her stockings and drew the silk back over her leg, buttoning them back in place. Even those little stitches that held the buttons were sensitive enough to send a little shiver up her back. He tied the ribbon tight around her thigh again, and then moved to the other leg.

By the time he had finished this, she was ready for more.

She fell asleep in his arms, staying so close to him that a flesh and blood woman might have felt crushed. She liked it when Grau's arms were around her, when his leg draped across hers. Her body had none of the restlessness of a flesh and blood person; she didn't care if she could barely even move. She felt so safe pressed against him like their bodies might become one during the night. Maybe it was something her soul had missed in this life, having never been carried by a mother…although she certainly didn't feel like Grau's child.

A small whisking sound in the early morning hours made her stir. She opened her eyes and saw, in the wan light of dawn, a figure sweeping the floor.

A Fanarlem servant. Servant or slave? The family always said 'servant', and by this Velsa supposed they might have been paid a wage, but just like her, they would have very little freedom even if they left.

The figure wore a long brown tunic and trousers with sturdy but well-worn shoes. It had hair made of long brown yarn, worn in a braid in what seemed almost a mockery of Daramon fashions.

Abruptly, as if it felt Velsa's eyes upon it, the thing turned and stared at her. Its glass eyes looked as real as her own, but the rest of its features were a crude imitation. It had no eyelashes, no lips, no nostrils—just two little black stitches on her nose to suggest them.

She couldn't even tell if it was male or female.

The stare in its eyes turned to a glare of hatred, the features contorting into such disgust that Velsa shut her own eyes against it. She pulled the blanket over her face. She didn't know what to do but hide.

Grau's arms didn't feel safe anymore.

That creature was her own kind. It looked nothing like her, but that was simply chance. She could have had its life; it could have had hers.

Maybe she should have counted her lucky stars or maybe she should have felt sympathy toward the thing, asked Grau where the servants lived and whether she might do something to brighten their days. Instead she felt only a bottomless horror. She never wanted to see the Fanarlem servant again.

CHAPTER SEVEN

A few days later, Grau and Velsa were playing a more serious game of chatrang, but they both looked up when a messenger stopped by with a letter for Preya.

"Senirin is having a dance," she said. "On Saturday. She says you're welcome to come too, Grau, before you go on patrol."

"Hmm."

Preya glanced at Velsa like, *See, there he goes.* "I know you don't like dances much, but it'll be your last chance to see your friends in town. Don't make me go alone."

"I can't leave Velsa home alone with Ma and Papa."

"Bring her, then!" Preya stretched onto her tip toes. She was not one for sitting still or even standing still. "It's not beyond the bounds of etiquette. You don't have a wife."

"I know, but no one else has a concubine in Marjon. It's such a city thing. I'm not sure how people will react."

"Since when are you one to care how other people react?"

"Since I have Velsa's feelings to protect."

"We'll both be there, and we'll both protect her," Preya said decisively. "You'll have to face this someday, unless you intend to never come home. Better to do it now."

Velsa dreaded the occasion herself, but hopefully the Thanneau siblings together would provide a buffer.

On Sunday afternoon, trying her best to ignore the anxious

fluttering inside her, Velsa donned the nicer dress Grau had purchased for her. It was a knee-length frock with a sash belt and loose long sleeves, worn with wool leggings. The colors were muted and reminded her of the marshes; a dark green for the tunic, and fawn for the leggings, but the sash was a rich blue.

"Let me do something with your hair," Preya said, inviting Velsa to sit before her bedroom mirror. Her bedroom was messy, strewn with shirts and socks. The cage for some probably long-dead pet sat in one corner. The walls were pasted with some pictures of actresses; humid air had rippled them.

"Are those actresses you fancy?" Velsa asked, letting just a little mischief into her tone, like she used to talk with the other girls at the House. She was quite comfortable talking to Preya by now.

"They're all the same one, actually. Contalla Prenzata. I saw her perform once, when Mama took me to Nisa. She can look a thousand different ways. It was actually seeing her that solidified my feelings in my own mind. It's well known that she's a lesbian, but she's an actress, so it doesn't matter. Actresses can do what they like."

"You have the freedom, that you *could* do something else."

Preya lifted Velsa's hair, revealing the entire length of her neck, so the golden band was plain to see. "Have you ever been without this?" she asked.

"Only for a minute, when my body was changed as I got older…"

"Such a little innocent looking thing you are." She let Velsa's hair fall down again, and brushed with careful strokes. "But I wonder if deep down you must hate us all."

"Of course I don't hate you." Velsa wasn't sure whether to be flattered or offended. Of course she didn't hate Grau and Preya…but she rather liked the suggestion that she *could*, that Preya credited her with having such dark and secret thoughts.

"We keep you captive."

"*You* don't."

"Grau does."

"You're not afraid of telepaths?"

"I am. And I know he's scared for you. He cares about you, and he feels deeply responsible for your welfare. He's never had a care in the world, before. You're good for him. But... doesn't it always hurt the soul to be under lock and key? Maybe there's no help for it, though." Preya opened a drawer and fished out the ornaments. "I don't think I'll do the buns again. Your hair is lovely framing your face. But maybe two little braids, crossed in the back, with some cloth flowers."

Preya wove two segments of Velsa's hair into plaits, her hands gentle as always. When this was done, Preya unpinned her own braids. Her hair fell past her waist, black and thick. If Velsa could grow her own hair, she would have enviable locks, too. Maybe Grau would be wealthy someday, and could buy her such hair.

"If you belonged to me, I would have to remove your band, just once, when we made love," Preya said. "To know what it felt like, to share my thoughts with someone else."

Velsa flushed. "You wouldn't be scared of sharing your thoughts?"

"Not with a concubine. I know you'd be hesitant to tell my secrets. It would make us a little closer to equal. And it would be a relief, to have one person who really knew me."

"Would you know my thoughts, too?"

"Maybe. I'm not sure how it works. It probably depends on how much control you have."

Not much, Velsa thought. Maybe it was for the best that Grau didn't remove the band. She didn't want him to know her thoughts. Most of her life, she rarely even thought about the band.

But it was beginning to feel tight and heavy around her neck. As if she had grown out of it, somehow.

Grau looked so handsome, dressed for the dance, in dashing black with his boots freshly polished. And Preya, too, with her hair in one loose braid woven with ribbons, and a crimson tunic and fur-edged cloak. Velsa was able to shove aside her nerves and all her troubled thoughts of telepathy and freedom.

They took the canoe into town, Grau weaving magic with his hands to speed the waters along while Preya paddled, so the ride was swift and smooth.

The night was on the early edge of sunset. Lanterns already blazed on the streets. The dance was held in the town meeting hall, a large wooden structure painted white with symbols of welcome painted on the doors and shutters: horseshoes and grapes. Music was already playing from inside; the formal dances popular in Atlantis. Velsa had been taught a few of the common ones at the House.

Inside, the room was warm from dozens of bodies and hundreds of candles, magnified by mirrors along the back wall. The band was in one corner, a bar at the other. People were dancing in sets of four, couples twirling around and then rejoining the square to hold hands, kick and clap in time with the music. Different drum beats signaled different moves, to aid anyone who forgot the steps.

Immediately, several people rushed forward to greet Grau and Preya. A pretty girl with curly hair kissed Preya's cheek in greeting, while Grau introduced Velsa to some other young men.

Their reaction was predictable by now. "Damn, Thanneau, she isn't bad looking." "I didn't know Fanarlem came that pretty." "What is it like?" They spoke as if she wasn't there.

"Please," Grau said. "She was worth every coin and then some and that's all you need to know."

"Ooh," one of them said.

"Grau!" Preya smacked his arm, turning away from her own cluster of friends. "What kind of response is that?"

"What? She means a lot to me."

"Well, your boorish friends are taking it the wrong way."

"Boorish?" One of them clutched his heart in mock offense. "We said she's pretty. What do you want?"

Now Preya's friends were starting to gather around Velsa

too. "She looks so real…" "She has fingernails!"

"That's enough," Preya said. She sounded uncertain now, whether this had been a good idea. "Velsa is pretty much a normal person. She could basically be Grau's wife."

"Grau's *wife?*" one short, snappy-eyed girl asked, sounding appalled.

"I mean, of course she isn't, but I'm just saying, it's not like she's slept with all kinds of men. She's eighteen and she can read and write and sew, and play chatrang, and anyway, she's just like us." Preya flung off her cloak as she spoke and cast about for the row of hooks where other coats and capes already hung.

"But…she's not," said the snappy-eyed girl. "She's a Fanarlem. She's supposed to be a servant."

"I don't want to talk about it anymore," Grau said. "She's not my wife, of course not, just the companion of my travels." He took Velsa's hand. "Let's dance."

He didn't join one of the squares—in fact, he didn't dance at all, but whisked her off to the other side of the room and poured himself a drink.

"Stars in the sky," he muttered. "I'm sorry, Velsa. I knew this was a bad idea. They're not close friends."

"It's how everyone sees me," she said.

"I know," he said, almost snappish.

"I mean, you don't have to be sorry. I'm used to it, I guess."

"You're not," he said. "I know you're not. I just feel helpless. I can't make you real…"

Velsa flashed back to Amleisa, all those months ago, saying that concubines had to embrace their fate, and not fight. She might have meant this, as much as anything. Maybe it would be easier if Velsa could just accept that no one would see her as a real person as soon as she stepped into public.

Grau put down his wine glass, now empty, and took her hand. He led her to join the dance. She tried to distance her mind from all the people around them, to see only him—even though worry lines creased his brow.

90

They clapped their hands together, and crossed paths, meeting back to back, before clapping again. The dance was slow enough that it was easy to follow, even if you didn't know the steps. They fell in with another couple, joining hands. The other man hesitated before he took Velsa's hand. The other girl looked at her curiously.

Velsa had told Grau she was good at controlling her emotions. Was it a skill so easily forgotten in a couple weeks of kindness? She smoothed her expression and reminded herself how she was fortunate to be here at all. It was likely that no other Fanarlem girl had ever walked in the front door of this hall except to clean the floors.

They shared two dances, and then some of Grau's friends returned, with brief apologies that perhaps they'd been a little crude. Now the men talked of business and Grau related the story of the Marnow farm.

While Grau's attention was caught elsewhere, one of the girls sidled up to Velsa and hissed, "You're no *wife*."

Velsa smothered an impulse to yank the girl's braids. She couldn't entirely suppress the venom in her eyes. She was so tired of being spoken to like this, but she had to endure it, over and over and over, as long as she lived.

Preya hurried over, pulling Velsa away.

"Maybe you should spend some time apart from Grau," she said. "Flirt with some other men if you can possibly stand it."

"What's going on?" Velsa shrank back.

"My big mouth," Preya said. "You know that girl Ellie? She met us at the door? In the blue dress?"

Velsa realized Preya meant the snappy-eyed girl. "Yes."

"She's been whispering around the room, that Grau treats you like a wife. And the thing is, she had a crush on Grau a few years back. He was barely even aware. I thought she was over it, but now I'm not so sure. I think she's jealous."

"I don't want to flirt with other men!"

"Fates, I don't want you to either. Maybe we should just leave. No, that's more suspicious. We'll just have to stick it out

91

and try our best to diffuse the rumor."

Now Preya drifted to the bar, but she chose the punch with lemon slices floating in it rather than the wine. She took a swig and offered the cup to Velsa. "Have a taste."

Velsa sipped the sweet liquid, which certainly was delicious, tasting mainly of fruit and only vaguely of spirits. If only she could enjoy the relaxing effect.

They were joined by the girl who had first greeted Preya. "My goodness," she said. "She can drink."

"Grau got her a spell," Preya said. She seemed edgy. "Velsa, this is my friend Senirin."

Senirin nodded to Velsa politely before turning to Preya. "I hope you're not avoiding me."

"Of course not. I was trying to stop Ellie from spreading nonsense about my brother."

"Oh, that." Senirin waved a hand. "It was nothing. She just can't quite get over him."

"I understand…" Preya spoke into her cup.

"I suppose you heard that I'm going to Atlantis early," Senirin said. "My grandmother invited me and my parents figure it's better to introduce me into society sooner rather than later."

"I heard," Preya said.

"I'm looking forward to seeing you there." Senirin smiled, in a half-hearted way.

"It's a ways off."

"A dance for old time's sake?"

Preya put down her cup as if defeated. She tilted her head toward Velsa. "Seems like Grau's winding down his conversation. Do you mind?"

"No, no," Velsa said.

Preya and Senirin joined hands and walked to the dance floor, without hardly looking at one another. But Velsa saw familiarity as much as shyness—that they knew one another's movements, and didn't need to check what the other was doing.

"Preya's first love," Grau said, stepping away from the one friend he was still conversing with. "But I'm glad Senirin is leaving. She's just a tease who breaks my sister's heart over and over."

"Preya said there's a girl here who likes you."

He squinted. "Ellie? I don't think she's serious."

"Did you ever court her?"

"Oh, no. I've danced with her here and there. I've never *courted* anyone. I don't share many interests with these women."

"If sharing interests was your priority, you certainly didn't know you'd get that with me."

"That's true, but I also knew you wouldn't get in the way. Any girl I might marry from Marjon would urge me to settle for my lot as the third son and a fish salesman. Sorcery isn't what people out here *do*."

Velsa watched Preya, who was beaming as she danced— but Senirin kept a distance. They didn't hold each other as the men and women did.

And around the room, glances turned frequently toward Grau. Velsa felt as if they were all talking about her.

Grau noticed them too. He still had that troubled crease in his brow.

"I should have followed my instincts and kept you home," he said. "It must seem like I'm flaunting the family wealth."

Preya rejoined them, but now her usual stride had deflated to a drag.

"Are you all right?" Grau asked.

She looked at him, her eyes shining wetly. "I'll be fine."

"It's for the best," he said. "She was using you. You bought her all those presents and what did she ever do for you?"

"You're not making me feel any better. What do you really know about relationships, Grau? Velsa has no choice but to be with you."

"I'm trying to comfort you, Preya! You think my relationship has been simple? More like a tragedy that I can't unsee."

Velsa stiffened, and he took her hand in a reassuring grasp as he continued, "Now that I know that Fanarlem think and feel

93

just as potently as we do, the whole world seems like an evil place, and I have no power to do anything about it. I can't free her. She has nowhere to go. I can't free the servants we have at home. Where would *they* go? And I can't go around telling everyone the truth. Most of them won't even believe me."

Preya's lashes shaded her eyes. "Oh, Grau," she said. "I'm supposed to be the pessimist between us."

None of them cared to dance, after that, but Grau insisted they stick it out a little longer so they didn't seem to be running off in shame.

Velsa wilted with relief when they finally made it back to the canoe. Grau and Preya both seemed a little drunk—they had made liberal use of the bar, to Velsa's dismay, since she wasn't strong enough to paddle the canoe all the way home by herself.

"You'd better not tip us over," Velsa said, when Preya stumbled to her seat.

"I'm okay. I just dunno the way home."

"I could navigate...these waters...in my sleep," Grau said.

"But you're not asleep. You're drunk," Velsa said. "So I hope you know what you're doing. It's cold out here, and remember, if I get wet, my stuffing will warp out of place."

Grau pulled himself together a little. "I'll get you home safe and sound, bellora. I promise."

Indeed, he had no trouble finding his way through the moonlit waters. Despite the damp cold, the marsh under a starry sky was one of the most beautiful things Velsa had ever seen. It was so very lonely, and she wanted nothing more than to be lost in a sea of shining, living grass, far away from the world, with the only two people she truly cared for. The dance seemed very small and inconsequential under the bowl of stars.

CHAPTER EIGHT

The next day, Grau's father came home from his daily business. He entered with furrowed brows, furious eyes, and a deadly quiet settled upon his shoulders like a mist.

"All of you," he said, "come to the dining room, *now*."

"What's wrong?" Grau's mother asked.

Grau's father was looking through the bookshelf, pulling out a stack of the pamphlets; the ones Grau had brought home and many others besides. He flipped through them until he found the one he was seeking, and then he went to the dining room.

They all had worried expressions, but Grau and Preya especially. Cold fear trailed down Velsa's spine.

"I need to read this to you all," Grau's father said. "'A Treatise on Fanarlem.'"

Grau put his arm around her.

"Grau, I wouldn't do that right now if I were you," his father said.

Grau only moved closer to her. "What is this about?" he demanded.

"What is this *about*? The entire town is talking about you and her. That's what it's about. They're saying you wish to have Velsa as your *wife*."

Velsa's arms tightened, almost involuntarily, around her waist. *Grau's father won't send me away,* she thought. *He paid for me. But what could he do? Sell me to someone else?* Her mind raced over

95

possibilities.

Preya dropped her head into her hand. "It's my fault," she said. "It was an offhand comment. I just didn't want the girls to see Velsa like she was a whore."

"Well, then, you were really stupid, Preya," Grau's father said. "I understand that Velsa is likable, but it doesn't matter if *you* like her. There are people in this town who would harm her and your brother if they thought he saw her as a wife. You can't take your friendship with Velsa outside of this house ever again."

In a strange way, Velsa wondered if he was trying to protect her. It didn't feel like any consolation. She watched the pamphlet waving in his hand.

"I have never regretted anything so deeply as offering Grau the gift of this girl," he continued. "I expected her to be servile, and she is not. I understand the temptation to welcome her into the family as if she is a whole person, but we all need to heed these words."

He opened the pamphlet. "'The race of Fanarlem was created centuries ago. Although the original intent was to create a better way of reviving the dead, the true and fated purpose of Fanarlem were soon revealed.

'Fanarlem bodies are fate's way of cleansing the evil in our souls. When Fanarlem are called to be born, the weakest souls are attracted to the call. These are the souls of sinners. These are the souls who have condemned themselves by the misdeeds of their past. But in becoming Fanarlem, they are granted a chance to save themselves with servitude.

'You may be tempted to feel pity or sorrow, when faced with the sight of the Fanarlem laborer. But remember, they brought this suffering upon themselves, and indeed, they do not suffer as you or I would. They feel no hunger, pain or cold. Their greatest pain is loneliness, but surely this is a fair burden for them to bear.

'The more a Fanarlem can adopt an attitude of agreeable servitude, the more they will find their work pleasant and their days easy to bear, and the sooner they will purify their souls for the next world. They will be reborn to greater happiness.

'No, do not pity the Fanarlem—only take them as a warning, to take care in your actions in this life.'"

He turned the page, as if to continue. Grau shoved his chair back and stood. "It isn't true," he said.

"You think you know more about how the world works than Lord Jherin?"

"Where is the proof?" Grau demanded. "Where is the *proof?*"

"Kalan Jherin is the Wodrenarune," his father said. "And Fanarlem *do* have damaged souls."

"And Miralem believe there is a goddess sleeping in the moon. We believe the fates speak to the Wodrenarune—well, I did believe it, but I'm not so sure anymore. Velsa isn't a condemned soul."

"There is no way you could possibly know that," his father said. "She has been given the guise of a pretty young woman, but we have no way of knowing what is in her soul. Sometimes I find the expression in her eyes to be quite rebellious."

"Stop it." Grau slammed his hands on the table. "I really don't care what Kalan Jherin says. I know what my gut says. I know the sinking feeling in my stomach that says I've done something wrong. I felt it when I bought her, and I felt it the other night when you told me I needed to bed her."

"You do need to bed her."

"Well, I *did*, all right? So *enough.*"

Preya's eyes widened.

Grau shook his head. "And even so, how do we know that souls are really purified by slavery?"

"Whether or not we choose to believe it, everyone in town will believe it. The law believes it. You can't talk of marriage and love. You can't bring Velsa to a gathering if she isn't going to behave with the submission everyone expects of her. You need to show your place versus hers. Have her fetch your drink, hold your drink. Reprimand her if she speaks out of turn." He stood. "It pains me to punish my children, but for your own good, you must remember this day. Velsa is spending the night in the servant's hut, and Preya, I will deal with you in a moment."

"Oh, Garen," Grau's mother said with distress, but she didn't intervene.

"The servant's hut?" Grau cried. "She doesn't belong in that dirty hovel."

"If you are really so concerned about the welfare of Fanarlem, then you can spend the night there with her," his father said. He stood and grabbed Velsa's arm. "I'm sorry, but it has to be this way. I'm not risking our wealth and safety over this."

He dragged her out of the room. After a few steps she picked up her pace, so he was not tugging on her. It was no use resisting.

Outside, the sky was full of stars and a moon that shone on the grasses. Tonight its solitary beauty was foreboding. He hustled her down a path and she kept tripping in the darkness. He led her to a one-room stone hut, barely in view of the house. From the outside, it was dark, and had no chimney.

He threw the door open. In a dim and drafty room, two Fanarlem sat at a table around a single candle, playing a game of cards. The one Velsa had seen sweeping Grau's floor was now smoking a cigarette. Just as Velsa could taste before she could eat, she supposed they could also smoke, although she had never seen such a thing. A bed stood on each side. Some gardening tools hung on the wall, and there was another table with a few books and baubles. The walls were painted pale pink with flowers, and that was about the only cheery thing about the place.

"She will stay with you tonight," Grau's father said. "Don't damage her. Her body is expensive."

He pushed her in with them and shut the door.

Velsa drew back against the wall. The two Fanarlem didn't say anything. Now that she could compare the two, she thought the one she had seen before was female. Her face and eyes had a softer, more feminine appearance.

"Sleep on the floor," the female one said. Her high voice

confirmed her gender, but her tone was harsh.

Velsa sat on the ground in the corner, trying to hide in the shadows.

"You're the youngest son's whore, aren't you?" the woman said.

Velsa shook her head, and then moved to the window. Where was Grau? Surely he wouldn't leave her here for long? She waited for long moments, watching the moonlit path.

Maybe she could find a place outside to go for the night... but the dew would seep into her skin, and insects might crawl between her stitches... Her stuffing was supposed to be repellent, but she didn't care to test that.

Even here, she wasn't sure she was safe from perils. The hut was clean, but it didn't feel inhabited, and the walls and doors and windows obviously weren't fitted tight. Maybe no place truly seemed lived in without flesh and blood people inside.

"Aren't you a whore, though?" the woman pressed after a while. "Do you think you're too fine to talk to us?"

"N-no," Velsa said. "Not at all. I would talk to you...I just didn't think you wanted me to."

"I'm not a pampered little bitch."

"We work hard for our redemption," the man added.

Velsa turned back to the window. She wasn't sure what she'd expected from the other Fanarlem. Empathy? Kinship? Then again, she'd been here for over a week and had never sought them out. She was much happier spending her days as part of a Daramon family. She didn't want to admit that she was afraid of them, that she found the sight of them repellent—it wasn't their fault, but it was true. They must sense her aversion. No wonder they hated her.

They kept playing cards as if she wasn't there at all. She heard them slapping down their moves, occasionally murmuring about their turns, the sound of their lips drawing on the cigarette as they passed it back and forth between them.

She waited, but outside there was only the lonely fields. She watched the moon climb the sky, placing all her focus on it. It seemed so far away.

One of the Fanarlem blew out the candle, plunging the room into darkness. They climbed into their beds without a word to her or each other.

"Are you going to sit down, girl?" the woman said. "Too accustomed to having pillows and feather mattresses wasted on your bones?"

"No..."

The woman threw off her blanket, coming right up to Velsa. "Yes, I saw you the other night, so pleased with yourself. Grau's little toy. I suppose you think I'm hideous. You're lucky the master told me not to damage you, and I heed my masters, or I'd carve your pretty face to shreds."

Velsa turned away, groping in the darkness for the door. She would rather wander all night than spend another moment here, if Grau wasn't coming. She couldn't believe he hadn't come.

The ground now had a light coating of frost, which sparkled in the moonlight. The wind was blowing steadily. She yearned for a cloak. The wind was harsh, almost painful on her cheeks.

She felt a little better when she stood between the hut and the house, and both were a distance away. Now, it was just her and the lonely land.

But it wasn't really lonely at all. She had felt all the life inside of it, holding the crystal. Grau had learned to feel it at any time. All of its whispers, all of its breath and warmth and memory, was still there whether she felt it or not.

She remembered the way he had drawn warmth from the hay that had spent time in the sun. She walked to the edge of the path, and held her hands out to the grass that stood chest-high, growing in shallow puddles.

"Help me," she whispered. "Can you hear me?"

The grasses sighed in the wind.

She looked up to the moon. "Am I really a cursed soul?"

The land and sky offered no answer, but she already felt that she had an answer for herself.

100

No. No, I am not.

If this was true, her life seemed a cruel joke. She thought of herself, pinned beneath Grau, how she felt not just desire but an intense hunger for safety. It was the best she could hope for, being Grau's possession. She believed that their connection was real, but it would always be tainted by circumstance.

The Fanarlem woman in the hut was so quick with her cruelty. And why not, if she had no comforts herself? Velsa might be bitter too. Being created to be desired had indeed given her a potential advantage. But would it end here? Could she be anything more than this?

What would it feel like to belong only to herself?

She wanted to smack Preya, that she would even consider marrying a man she couldn't be attracted to, when she might go to Nalim Ima and build her own life—a choice Velsa could never have.

She didn't want to go any closer to the house, so she turned down a path and began to wander, knowing she might get lost. It didn't seem frightening, to be lost. She couldn't die that way. It was the cities that would harm her—the people. Not the wilds. She briefly imagined what it would be like to simply disappear into the marsh, to live endlessly. She would know every inch of it, eventually; she would be able to do sorcery here without a crystal. People in the town would spot her, once in a while, before she disappeared, and they would tell legends about her. They might think she was a nature spirit over time.

The plants and the waters, the toads and snakes and birds, were all beautiful.

But they could not offer her friendship.

And besides, she thought, her thoughts turning practical, *it's too wet out here.*

Still, she wandered. It wouldn't hurt to be lost for a time.

She wasn't sure how long it had been when she heard someone running. She turned and saw a light in the distance, the way she had came.

She crouched in the grasses, ready to hide, but as the voice got closer, it called her name.

She stood up again. "Grau?"

"What are you doing out here?" He ran to her and pulled her into an embrace. "Velsa, I thought you ran away." He stopped. "Maybe you are running away."

"Not from you. But where *were* you?"

"I'm sorry I didn't come after you right away. Preya was crying and my mother was yelling and Agrin was telling me I'd better not mess with Papa right now and—well, then I did come and you were gone. I've been frantic trying to track you." He spread his hand on the back of her head, still clutching her close. "I don't believe it. I don't believe all those things about Fanarlem souls. I'm sorry I ever believed it."

"I'm not. You wouldn't have ever bought me if you didn't believe it."

"I'm going to prove it's not true."

She looked at him uncertainly. "How?"

"I don't know yet, but there must be some way."

She didn't really believe him. "I'm not sure it would matter. How many people would want it to be true? What about all the other Fanarlem? What could be done with them?" She smoothed his jacket. "It's enough for me to know that you believe it."

"I'm taking you away tonight," he said. "We would be leaving soon anyway. I know my father is trying to protect the family but he should never have said all that to you. Still…we'll have to be careful. I can't expect we'll find better attitudes anywhere else we go."

"I understand," she said soberly, taking one glance back at the endless expanse of land and sky before taking his hand. It was only in places like this that she could truly be free.

"Did you really have a sinking feeling in your stomach when we made love?" she asked, as they galloped off on Fern's back into the night. Someone must hear them, she thought, but no one came out to stop them. "Because truly I forgot all about your father before long."

"I did too, in the moment," he said. "But I thought about it later that night."

"Will Preya be all right?"

"Papa will give her ten lashes," he said. "But he wouldn't really hurt her."

"Won't he?"

"I mean, he'll hurt her a little, but that's just how it is. She won't bleed. I suppose you were never physically punished at the House, huh? It wouldn't do much."

"They took our hands away if we broke the rules."

"I think I'd rather have the lash."

"I don't know." Velsa shrugged. "It meant you couldn't do any needlework or read, but otherwise it hardly seemed to matter. There wasn't much to do."

"I guess I see what you mean. If you didn't have to eat or use the privy or even change clothes, you wouldn't need your hands as much as I would."

"If you were really bad, they'd sew your mouth shut, and that I'd mind, but it never happened to me. I was good. Most of the time. Not always good on the inside but I knew to stay quiet."

"If only Preya had that quality," he said, but he sounded more admiring than upset.

"I'm so sorry I couldn't say goodbye to her."

"We'll see her again."

CHAPTER NINE

They didn't travel the same way they had come, but veered north. He pulled out another large map and pointed to their final destination: a small military outpost in the hills to the northwest, right on the border of the Miralem nation of Otare.

"They try to be pretty strict with border crossings these days," he said, "but you can't keep out Miralem telepaths who want to make money. The border towns always have a higher concentration of telepaths who will slip over here for a few days, make some money, and go back to their own hoity-toity nation."

"Are they that bad? Apparently I used to be one of them in my past life, you know."

"They're not that bad, if you like them feeling out your emotions, and going on about their goddess. The one who sleeps in the moon and wakes up when they need her, which apparently is never in all of recorded history. Except sometimes she sends her children, who supposedly happen to be the palest of Miralem, the ones who look the least like Daramons."

"I really don't like people," Velsa sighed.

"Well, we need one, in this case. A Miralem person. I want to get a reading on your soul and see if it's damaged."

She tensed. "And what if it *is*?"

"I've heard that some Miralem can repair souls. So we'll ask. Either way, I don't believe that you should suffer for it. And if I'm wrong, may the fates bring us both back as Fanarlem together."

"Don't say that," she said, thinking immediately of the Fanarlem man and woman in the hut. "Don't tempt a curse on our heads."

"Never." He kissed the top of her head. "With this in mind, we may be sleeping in more barns. I want to save my money."

The travel was grueling at times, the long days on Fern's back, the weather turning colder by the day—and the mile—as their path led northward. Passing through small towns and hamlets along the route, she was a novelty and everyone stared, so she learned quickly to wear her hooded cloak at all times. They were comfortable alone, if sometimes a bit pricked from the beds of hay in their humble accommodations.

When they rested together after a long day, Grau would kiss her or stroke her thigh, and in another moment they were tangled together. She felt safe now, when he was inside her, with every affirmation of his need for her and every tender kiss and caress. His body felt like a shield against the horrors of the world, against which they stood.

They came, at last, to the larger town nearest his post, with a few days to spare. The town was nested between hills, with a river flowing beneath it—not the Atlantis River but one of its tributaries, the Sirian River, which marked the border between Atlantis and Otaré. The architecture looked different than in Nisa; more vertical, as if to compete with the surrounding hills. Spires marked the important buildings. Even the houses were often four narrow stories tall. She realized perhaps the steep surrounding land must be difficult to build upon, hemming in the town.

There was also a town on the Miralem bank of the river, although it was smaller, more of a village. Guard posts lined the water on both sides.

Here, Grau found a proper inn to keep Fern while they looked for a telepath.

"How do you find the telepaths?" Velsa asked. "What do

Miralem look like?"

"Around here, they don't look very different from us. Anyway, I think they find us. All we need to do is walk around and think about needing their services."

"They can feel us thinking about them?"

"If they're good at what they do."

This brought home the Daramons' fear of telepaths more than anything else Velsa had heard.

They walked down streets paved smooth. Grau kept staring at them. "They use sorcery to smooth the rock," he said. "It's difficult magic, but they must be good at it up here, with all those rocks on the hillsides."

The pavement made the entire town seem more tidy. It was a quaint place, with lots of shops to peer into. Grau stopped in a particularly enticing candy shop offering all sorts of small confections made of nuts and nut pastes, candied flowers, honeycomb and chocolate.

As Grau took out coins to purchase a few choice selections, she considered for the first time what it would be like to carry a pouch of money herself and decide to buy things. She quickly squelched the thought. She could never ask Grau for any money of her own unless his income far exceeded her price.

When they had reached the edge of town, just when they were beginning to wonder if they would have any luck, a woman in a cloak slipped out of an alley and stood before them. "Are you seeking something?" she asked.

"Yes," Grau said, with a touch of relief. "Someone who can read souls."

"I can. For the girl? A half-piece."

She led them back down the alley and up exterior stairs. They were creaky and offered an open view of their increasing height behind each step. Velsa felt a little dizzy as they climbed.

They entered a small room, sparsely decorated, as Grau held her hand tightly.

The woman hung up her cloak. Her dress was deep blue with embroidered sleeves and skirt, and her blonde hair hung long and loose. Grau said the Miralem here looked like Daramons, but Velsa had never seen anyone with pale hair before.

"Take off your cloak, madam," the woman said. "This won't take long, but it helps if I can see your face."

No one had ever called Velsa 'madam' before, unless she counted Grau teasing her in the bedroom.

"A golden band," the woman said, drawing her hands to her chest with a look of revulsion.

Velsa touched her neck, but her collar still covered the golden band as it always did. The woman must have read it from her face, somehow.

"You have fond feelings for her, sir," the woman said. "And yet you keep her locked up."

"For her safety."

"For *yours*," she said.

"Fanarlem telepaths are not well regarded," he said.

"Not in *your* country." She took Velsa's hand. "He's afraid of your power."

Velsa looked at Grau uncertainly.

He gave his head a brief shake, brows furrowed.

"He's afraid you'll read his mind."

"I wouldn't," Velsa said. "I don't even know how."

"I'm not afraid of *you*," he insisted. "I just—I don't trust telepathy, all right? None of it. And no wonder. I didn't ask to have my mind read now. All I want is to know if Velsa's soul is damaged."

"Let's see…" The woman took Velsa's other hand too, and turned them both so her palms faced the ceiling. She held Velsa's hands lightly, her skin unnaturally warm for such a cold day. She shut her eyes. Velsa wasn't sure what to do so she shut her eyes too. It was easier than looking at Grau, who still seemed upset.

"Only a bit," the woman pronounced.

"A bit?" Grau said. "What does that mean?"

"All Fanarlem are born with damaged souls," the woman said. "That is simply a fact, likely caused by their forced creation.

Even when a flesh and blood person chooses to become a Fanarlem, their soul suffers for it slightly. It doesn't mean anything; it's a protective mechanism. A damaged soul experiences diminished emotions, which makes it easier to cope with trauma. Her soul will heal with experiences, especially with feelings of happiness, safety and security. Though I know those are in short supply for Fanarlem here."

"Is that really true?" Velsa asked.

"Of course it's true. I hope he hasn't told you anything different." The woman didn't seem to trust Grau at all.

"No, *he* hasn't…but he's about the only one."

"Well…" The woman's expression softened just a little. She took one of Grau's hands along with one of Velsa's, like she was a link between them. "You keep that up, sir. Her scars will heal with care. But I'd start by taking off that band. Would you make her go through life blindfolded? Telepathy is a power but more than that, it is a sense—an essential part of life."

"Not for us," Grau said. "Not for Daramons." He paid her with a slightly curt thanks.

"You really think I would read your mind?" Velsa asked, as they went down the stairs.

"She said that. I didn't." But then he sighed. "Not on purpose. But maybe by accident. Telepaths can do strange things when they get emotional. Like I said before, you won't necessarily have control."

"I have no training. And what do you think I'd learn?"

"It's not that I'm hiding anything," he said. "But would you want me reading *your* mind?"

"No…I wouldn't want anyone reading my mind."

"That woman, there—I could feel her brushing across me, searching for something she could accuse me of. Not an experience I care to repeat anytime soon."

"Do all Miralem read minds?"

"No, only the skilled ones can, but—"

"Then I wouldn't."

"Maybe not at first, but, you might start to read my

emotions without realizing. Look how you healed Fern in a panic. You definitely have talent, if not skill."

"And good thing!" she exclaimed. "Grau, I think I already know your emotions by now. The good ones and the bad ones." She crossed her arms and pressed her lips together, trying to suppress anger.

"Look," he said, "there's nothing I can say about it. I trust you—"

She turned at the bottom of the stairwell. "Then—please—take off my band! If only for a night…"

"I don't trust *telepathy*. I can't do it, Velsa. It might hurt much more when I have to replace the band, and—we're headed into a camp where a telepathic concubine is completely unacceptable." He put a hand on her shoulder.

"I was born with this power, and I've never even known how it feels."

Stop this, she told herself. Her feelings for him surely couldn't crumble this easily, but she was surprised at how painful it was to hear him deny her this. Why did she need to defy him? She had never defied Dalarsha, and she loved and trusted Grau more.

"I'm teaching you sorcery, for just that reason—so you *will* have power of your own." He huffed, raking a hand through his hair. "The telepath wasn't as costly as I expected. How about if I buy you a crystal?"

A crystal…

It didn't feel like enough, when she had other powers, powers granted to her by fate. But she also yearned for a crystal, to be able to tap into the greater forces around her at any time.

She could settle for it.

She had to, really. What else could she say?

It was getting dark now, but it got dark early at this time of year, and the shops were still open. Lamplighters were going around tending to the oil lamps, but magic lights beamed at corners and from shop windows, casting more powerful illumination. The little town was a glowing gem at night, nested between the dark swell of the hills.

The magic shop occupied the ground floor of one of the narrow buildings. Inside, between shelves lined with potions and books, was a glass display case containing crystals. Some were no larger than a pea, often set in earrings or rings. The largest one was half of a split geode almost as large as her head, a sparkling little cavern of smoky crystals.

"Can I help you, sir?" asked the shopkeeper, a genial-looking Daramon man who was unremarkable except for the bluish color of his eyes. Perhaps he had Miralem blood.

"We're looking for a small crystal for the lady," Grau said.

"A good idea," the shopkeeper said gently. "I know the world can be a dangerous place for anyone in your position. My sympathies."

Velsa didn't quite understand until Grau said, "Well, she's been a Fanarlem since she was young but I just want her to feel safe."

The shopkeeper thought she was flesh-born, and Grau was letting him think it. Maybe others had suspected it, but this was the first time someone had said so outright. It made her feel like an impostor, on the brink of being exposed and humiliated—and yet, how quickly she could get used to being treated like a Daramon girl, as the man started asking questions about their budget and interest, addressing them both equally.

He took out a tray with a dozen crystals in their price range. "Try picking them up," he said. "You're looking for one that sings to you."

In truth, they all sang a little. She heard faint sounds when she held them, like buzzing or the chime of bells. She chose the one she liked the best, an elongated shard with a golden tint and a haunting low song. Grau had the crystal-seller mount it on a chain so she could wear it close all the time.

Grau fastened it around her neck.

"You have a lovely girl," the man said in a kindly way that made it obvious he thought she was Grau's wife or, at the least, his potential wife. "Bless you both."

110

"I do indeed," Grau said, obviously pleased.

She was disappointed to find that wearing the crystal against her skin didn't produce a constant connection with the elements around her.

"Only when you concentrate, I'm afraid," Grau said. "Maybe it would be too distracting if you felt all those energies constantly. Still, I'm sure activating it will become second nature in no time."

They returned to their room, with baked potatoes for dinner, bought in one of the shops. After they had eaten, Grau took out his parcel from the candy shop.

"We'd better enjoy these," he said. "I don't think they'll give us candy in our military rations. And tonight, we should celebrate, now that we know that your soul is just a few happy moments away from being whole…" He opened a jar of honey and scooped out a dab, lifting the golden sweetness to her lips.

She sucked the honey from his finger. It tasted of summer flowers.

She dipped her finger into the jar and lifted it to his mouth, but at the last minute she put it on her own tongue instead.

"You little minx!"

She stuck out her tongue, the honey still held there.

He chased her tongue back into her mouth with his own, to give her a honey-flavored kiss. They leaned back onto the bed, as his hand freed the clasps of her tunic.

"This is the only time I wish you were a flesh and blood woman," he said. "With a warm, wet mouth." Although he was gazing at her fondly as he said it, she felt a little pang of jealousy.

"Have you kissed many flesh and blood women?" she asked.

"Not many." He paused. "A few village girls, at dances and the like. The Perfume Woman my father allowed me to see when I came of age."

Velsa knew from House gossip that it was common for fathers to take their sons to a courtesan when they came of age— a flesh and blood woman, of course—one who was particularly trained in teaching young men how to please a woman before he married. It was a matter of shame for a Daramon man to marry without any sexual experience, while for women it was just the opposite.

"But I still want you, just as you are, and only you. Every time I touch you, I know you a little better, and I love you a little more…"

She ran her hand through his hair—unruly from their travels—and gave him a soft smile. Her soul, surely, must be growing stronger, as safe as she felt right now. But she didn't say anything back. It was one of a concubine's few privileges, to be adored and keep an air of mystery about her own feelings.

He expertly unbuttoned her boots with his button hook and slid them off her legs, her pants and chemise following. He kissed her neck and trailed down to one of the nipples of her small breasts, where his teeth barely grazed the skin. She moaned with delight, closing her eyes.

Suddenly she felt his finger run a smear of honey from her navel down between her folds.

She sat up. "Grau! My skin isn't waterproofed on my stomach! Or…honey-proofed. You're going to make a mess!"

"Oh…"

"Well, lick it up—quick—"

His tongue ran down her stomach and tickled so that she couldn't help a spasming little laugh that was surely not the mood he had meant to set. She almost kicked him in the head on accident. He grabbed her feet to save himself.

"You're right," he said. "It's sort of soaked into you." He quickly got up and went to the wash basin, coming back with a wet cloth to dab her skin.

"It was a good idea in theory," she said, still recovering from the giggles. "But let's keep it to our mouths."

"Velsa," he said, pulling her body close against his now, her legs straddling him. "I want you to be my wife."

Her laughter grew a little more pained, despite an inner surge of joy. "I would love to be your wife."

112

His gazed pierced her with its sudden intensity. "There is a way it might happen, someday...," he said. "If you had been born a flesh and blood woman, you would be a legal citizen."

"But I haven't..."

"But we might be able to buy papers that say you were... Of course, we would have to move far from home, where no one would know us."

She felt shaky. "How much does such a thing cost?"

"I'm not sure. But if you were my wife and everyone around us thought you had been born flesh, you'd be treated like a real person. No one would think you needed to be servile, that your soul was corrupt."

"Grau..." Now she fought back a sob. She didn't dare hope such a thing might be possible. "But what about...the marshes? I thought you were worried about the land being sold. How could you protect it?"

"I don't love the marshes more than you. I will have to hope they can wait," he said. "I'll save every coin I can from here on out, and maybe when my patrol is over we could go to the city and see what we can find on the black market."

CHAPTER TEN

A few days later, they ventured outside of town to the base, for Grau to report for his patrol duties. Even from a distance, Velsa could see vast banners streaming from poles, displaying the flag of Atlantis and the emblem of the the Wodrenarune: a black wing spread against crimson.

A simple fence delineated the camp; it wouldn't keep out intruders, but there was no point in fences anyway against an enemy that could get inside your head. Still, the fence had a gate where Grau showed his papers as well as the papers that marked her as a concubine—the only woman allowed into military camps. Inside the fences stood a large two-story wooden building, a large box of a structure with a thatched roof. Surrounding this were stables, a few smaller wooden sheds, tents grouped around campfires, and a row of latrines. The men were mostly in a state of semi-leisure at the moment, polishing knives, eating from tin plates, talking, smoking. Although it was cold, some of them only wore undershirts with their military-issue gray pants. They looked like a crude lot, muscular in the way of laborers, unshaven and unwashed. And they all stared at her, despite her cloak.

"Another concubine," one man called, with an approving tone.

Did someone else have a concubine?She glanced around, worried. She missed the other girls at the House, but some of them were prone to jealousy. Another concubine might easily sniff out Grau's love for her and get them both in trouble.

They took Fern to the stables and entered the headquarters. Inside, they were greeted with a bow by a handsome man with dark brown skin and trim black hair cut short and sleek around his ears. He wore the same odd uniform as the men they had encountered in the barn, with the jacket short and tight.

"Grau Thanneau," he said, taking Grau's papers. "And his concubine. I'd advise you to not let her out of your sight if she means anything to you."

"I expect the other men will at least respect my girl?"

"Um, they should, but…I still wouldn't dangle out any temptations. They get lonely and bored and conduct is not held to much of a standard." He looked vaguely exasperated. "I'm Lieutenant Dlara, and glad to see you. You're to be our camp sorcerer."

"Yes, sir."

Lieutenant Dlara waved them toward an elegant table being used as a desk. The fine veneer of the dark wood seemed out of place among the bare wooden walls dressed up only by a few banners. "And I see your family is a member of the Agricultural Guild."

"We raise fish, actually," Grau said. "But we're not in the Fisherman's Guild because we farm them in a lake."

"Really. Farming fish. Never heard of such a thing. Well, it sounds like you're a long way from home, but always let me know if you need anything. You have a bed upstairs in the barracks in room 4, and your uniform and kit is waiting there for you."

"I'm sleeping in the barracks?" Grau asked. "I thought I'd have a tent. Is it a private room?"

"No, you're four to a room. We could set up a cot for…" He glanced at Velsa's paper. "For Velsa, if you find the bed too small. We could give you a tent if you insist, but it gets cold. I'd keep the bed, and as for privacy, well, you'll find a way. Or if you're Lieutenant Archel, you won't even care about privacy…"

115

Lieutenant Dlara sounded exasperated again.

"He has a concubine as well?" Grau asked. Obviously he had been curious too.

"Yes. She plays the flute for us many evenings." His tone didn't suggest that he enjoyed these concerts, however.

Velsa thought the girl must be one of the entertainer concubines, then. Or else, like Velsa, she didn't play an instrument well, but it was good enough for bored soldiers.

Lieutenant Dlara and Grau went over some paperwork. Velsa watched low flames cracking in the fireplace behind the lieutenant, trying not to dread living at this camp, with so many men. Lonely and bored men. No place for a lady, no place for a wife, so it was just a stark reminder that she was neither.

Next, they checked out their room, which was spartan— four beds that were hardly more than cots themselves, each neatly made with a pillow and a gray wool blanket. Three of the beds had pictures tacked on the wall and books on the nightstand, and one had a pack and a folded uniform atop the blanket, which must be intended for Grau.

Grau took his uniform into the adjacent washroom.

When he emerged, Velsa tilted her head, trying to decide if she liked the strange garment, which was almost identical to Lieutenant Dlara's. She was used to seeing Grau in a tunic, with a trim waist but a relaxed fit around his neck and arms, and a hem that fell just past his knees. This new jacket fit close, buttoning straight down the front to a leather belt with a metal buckle fastener at his waist. A jaunty gray cap completed the ensemble.

He tugged at the neck. "This damn thing's itchy. And tight."

"You don't wear any armor? You don't look a thing like the soldiers in books..."

The jacket was short enough that she saw the shape of his thighs, although the pants fit a little more loosely than the jacket, and still tucked into his usual boots.

"What are those for?" she asked, pointing at his shoulders. His jacket had small panels that buttoned down. "A hidden pocket of some kind?"

"It's called an epaulet," said another man, poking his head around the corner. "And it doesn't do anything, just decoration. The palace guard at Nalim Ima have been dressing like it for years. Latest fashion there. They're new uniforms."

He came in and shook Grau's hand. "I'm Ralaran Parvel," he said. "But people just call me Rawly."

"Grau Thanneau."

"And who is this charming creature?"

"Velsa," Grau said.

Rawly bowed. "What do you think of the uniforms, Velsa?"

"Handsome," she said. "But what will protect him from arrows?"

Rawly laughed. "What moldy epic have you been reading? The Ten Thousand Man Sacrifice is what protects him from arrows."

"Still, he could be hurt and in pain, all for the sake of not wearing a little armor?"

Rawly shrugged. "Lord Jherin says armor isn't necessary anymore. Adds weight."

"Are you doing a six month stint as well?" Grau asked.

"Two years, my friend, and then they've promised me a stable position in Atlantis. I'm halfway through already, although it's hard to believe. I thought we might have more action. This job is a snooze."

"That bad? I thought bandits caused trouble here and there."

"Once in a while." Rawly made a face.

"No dragon?"

"So you've heard the rumors too? Well, I haven't seen one."

It was a funny world, Velsa thought, when you wanted bandits to attack just for something to do.

"Can I offer you a tour of the grounds?" Rawly asked.

"Of course," Grau said.

Downstairs, Rawly stopped to bow to Lieutenant Dlara as

117

they passed his desk.

"Ah, good, Rawly," he said. "You take those two under your wing, will you?"

"Of course, sir," Rawly said. "Pleasure's all mine."

"He might be a bit of a flirt," Lieutenant Dlara told Velsa, "but you can trust him."

"Thank you, sir." Velsa wondered if they might be so lucky as to have friends.

There was something vaguely troubled in Lieutenant Dlara's eyes, but he moved the conversation on. "You'll have tests tomorrow, Thanneau. Thank the fates you're here. We've been short on sorcerers. Of course...oh, don't think I don't see that look in your eye, Rawly. Not much has happened in a while, it's true. It hardly matters whether we have sorcerers or flute-players when all we do is plod around. But you never know."

"The lieutenant seems like a good soul," Grau said, as Rawly showed them along.

"He's from the islands," Rawly said, which was explanation enough. People from the Balumi Islands just south of Atlantis were known for being good-natured. "Nah, I expect if you have to worry about anyone, it's Lieutenant Archel. He has a concubine too, and he likes all the attention she receives. I'm not sure if he'll appreciate a younger soldier having one."

"I certainly don't have Velsa with me for attention."

"What made you decide to buy her?"

"I wanted a companion for my travels." Grau glanced at her. "I wasn't really sure if I'd go through with it, though, until the minute I saw her."

"That's downright romantic," Rawly said.

Grau shrugged. He seemed to realize he risked saying too much. She guessed that Grau was not used to hiding his feelings. Preya said he didn't have a care in the world until Velsa came along. Not long ago, he would have been free to live any life he wanted. Now, he faced giving up his family and the place he loved, all for her.

It was hard not to feel guilty, although she also wondered if perhaps this might be his fate, the fate he had brought upon himself when he went to her House thinking it would be simple to buy her, that she was really a Perfumed Ribbon and not a woman.

Unless it was true in the end, and they were both deluding themselves, and she was a tainted soul after all. It wasn't always easy to believe her own heart over all the lectures she had been given.

In the evening, they dined at a long table with Rawly and Lieutenant Dlara, and the other men of higher rank and from better families.

Grau dined, anyway. She wasn't given a place at the table, but had to sit on his lap if she wanted to be there, which of course she did. Grau, certainly, would not have left her alone in the barracks after all the warnings.

Not far away sat Lieutenant Archel with his own concubine on his lap. She looked a little different from Velsa, because she was from a different House, which would have its own Fanarlem maker with their own style of faces. But she was similarly petite and pretty, with shoulder-length black hair, although it was more curled than Velsa's. Her face had a sleek look, with long eyelashes and an unusually full mouth. Her maker must have been especially skilled at lips, but it looked strange to Velsa. Her body also had a more voluptuous shape, with round breasts large enough to push into cleavage above the edge of her robe.

She didn't stay on Archel's lap for long. He said something to her, and she stood and picked up a flagon of wine from a side table. She strolled around the table with a slinking grace, filling glasses. Some of the men watched her and she lingered longer with the ones who did. Velsa saw one of them squeeze her rear and she said nothing.

She came to Grau and Velsa. "Would you like to help me serve?" she asked Velsa.

"I'd rather she didn't," Grau said.

"Don't be selfish, Thanneau," Lieutenant Archel said. "My little flower has been doing the work on her own for a long time."

"It's all right, Grau," Velsa said softly. "I don't mind. I'll be right here." It seemed safer not to argue, and she wasn't sure it was any better to be stuck on his lap staring at his meal.

But then she regretted it, because once all the wine glasses were full and none of the men seemed to need anything more, the other concubine began to stroll the table and let herself be pulled onto another man's lap. She laughed and whispered in his ear, and he stroked her hair and then put his hand on her breast. She pushed him away, but not seriously. The hand returned.

Velsa backed up against the wall. Memories of those two weeks in the House, before Grau rescued her, flashed through her mind. *Never again…*

Grau put down his napkin and turned in his chair, quietly motioning for her to return to him. His arm went back around her and he smeared some butter on his bread, then handed it to her.

Oh, Grau, you shouldn't!

He wasn't being careful.

Lieutenant Archel was looking at her curiously, and she put the bread down without a bite.

"Does your girl *eat?*" Lieutenant Archel asked.

"Sometimes."

"Look at this, my little flower! The girl *eats.* Eat something," he prompted Velsa.

Now the 'little flower' was giving her an expression that was neither interested nor fond.

Lieutenant Dlara cleared his throat. "This is a lot of fuss at the dinner table over nothing. Dinner ought to be an opportunity for us to reflect on our thoughts and observations."

"I thought you guys from the islands were supposed to be fun," Lieutenant Archel said. "Besides, what thoughts and observations? Nothing happens around here."

Other men grumbled agreement.

"Not everything is about battles and bandits," Dlara said. "I was just reading the latest paper from Atlantis and apparently

120

all sorts of imports from Nalim Ima are beginning to flood in to the mainland. The price of books published in Nalim Ima has gone down so much that people have been buying them by the dozen. The shops can't keep them in stock. Hardbound books with color plates, mind you, not just pamphlets. Can't wait for supply to catch up to these parts…"

"Yes, Dlara, we all know you've been to Nalim Ima," Archel said, like he hadn't really been listening at all.

Velsa finally dared to nibble on her bread. She could still feel the other concubine's eyes on her—what was her name, even?—but Velsa tried not to look at her.

She still knew, however, that the other concubine continued her rounds, spending time with any man who beckoned her. Of course she must know them all by now, since Grau seemed to be the only newcomer at the table. Only certain men were interested. Lieutenant Dlara ignored her completely, and Rawly was just shoveling food in his mouth like a starving man.

She could tell Grau was getting tired of her weight on his leg, but he didn't complain. She made the bread last a long time so he wouldn't feel compelled to give her any more of his food.

Near the end of the meal, the other concubine returned to Lieutenant Archel's lap, her clothes somewhat disheveled by now, so that Velsa could see almost her entire right breast beneath the loose hem of her undergarment, in the shadow of her robe.

Velsa wasn't even wearing her concubine's robes and she didn't know when she ever would, especially considering that Grau was trying to save money. With her arms and legs protected under sturdy clothes, her skin would stay clean and last a long time.

By the time the meal ended, it was dark outside, and fires were lit around the camp. "You two should stick around," Rawly said, when Grau's steps pointed to the barracks. "We have music after dinner."

"I guess it depends on who's making the music," Grau said. "If it's Archel's concubine, I'm not interested. I think you're right—we'd better stay away from them as much as possible."

"Well, it *is* her," Rawly admitted. "But not *just* her. Some of the men play too. If we ask nicely maybe Dlara will play his harmonica. He's shy about it, but it's something else. He got it in Nalim Ima. It looks like a strange little rectangular flute but he plays the best songs I've ever heard on it. Besides, if you avoid Archel forever you'll also miss the best of camp social life."

Grau's curiosity obviously got the better of him. "All right. We'll stay for a few minutes."

"You'd have to deal with it sooner or later," Rawly said. "But I'll stick with you. He can't hurt Velsa. Lieutenant Dlara would never allow it, anyway. He already disapproves of how Archel treats Flower."

"That's her name?" Velsa asked. Flower was usually just a nickname.

"We call her that. Her real name is something else, like… Sibalora? I can't remember. Something like that. Archel just calls her by nicknames and everyone else has pretty much settled on Flower."

Sibalora had such a different sound than Flower. One was a real name and one was a pet. A pang of sympathy swept through Velsa. That could have been her, or any of the girls at the House. She wondered about Amleisa and Nraya. Were they still called by name?

The men were gathered around a comfortable, crackling fire; not so blazing that it frightened Velsa. There was a horror story back in the House about a concubine long ago whose hair had caught on fire and her face had burned away, and when her replacement face finally arrived she looked like an entirely different girl. Velsa never knew if that story was true, and her skin was gently fireproofed, but better not to take chances. She also stayed away from the smoke, as the smell would cling to her for a long time.

Flower was already playing a song on the flute, to the slow beat of two drums. The song sounded similar to "Farewell to Sailors", which Velsa used to practice on the bastir, but the

122

melody was different in the chorus. When the other concubine had finished a few verses, one of the men took up the song with a strong, deep voice. Flower lowered her flute. She gyrated her hips to the pounding of the drums.

"Come here, doll," one of the men said. She drew a handkerchief from her pocket and fluttered it in his direction. He swatted at it playfully until he caught it, and pulled her against him. She stood straddled across his legs and rubbed her pelvis against his face.

Flower's dance was just one small interaction in the large circle of men; many of them were not even paying attention to her. But Velsa had a hard time seeing anything else. She had never witnessed anything so improper in public.

Rawly covered her eyes.

"Hey!" she exclaimed with surprise.

"Grau, I think your girl would blush if she could. You'd better keep her home and give her some dolls to play with, and I don't mean that kind."

"I'm not a kid," Velsa said.

"There's virgin and then there's innocent. You can be one and not the other." Rawly draped one arm around each of them. "Tell you what, I'll insist Dlara play that harmonica and take this evening out of the den of vice. But I can't save you every night."

As he left, Grau turned to Velsa. "Why do I get the feeling that now that we're here, and everyone has told us how boring it is, a murderous band of river pirates is going to show up within the week?" He frowned. "I'm not sure the border guard is for me."

"Bored already?" she teased.

"Not bored. Uneasy."

Velsa patted his arm, but she didn't know what to say. She was uneasy herself, and kept watching Flower, even as she tried not to. Flower had a seductive smile on her face, but Velsa thought her eyes were dead.

Rawly was chatting with Lieutenant Dlara, pointing back at them. Dlara nodded and took a silver object from his pocket. The man performing now wrapped up his song with a final chorus, and bowed to Dlara.

Dlara shook his dark head sheepishly. "Just a tune for my new squad sorcerer, Grau, and his girl, Velsa."

The harmonica was silver with engravings on the case and looked more like a small jewelry box than an instrument. She didn't expect the noise and energy that came out. It was a harsh sound, almost like someone wailing, but simultaneously more cheerful than any song she had grown up hearing. The men started clapping along almost immediately.

They sang, "Oh, I come on down the river with a bastir on my knee! I'm going to Atlantis, my true love for to see. It rained all night as I depart, though the clouds were dry, the sun so hot I froze to death, Su-za-na dry your eyes…Oh Su-za-na, oh don't you cry for me, I come on down the river with a bastir on my knee!"

They sang with great gusto and the bouncing beat was infectious. The drummers came in and the men were not just clapping but stomping their feet. Grau took her hand and spun her around, which made them cheer.

The songs of Atlantis and its neighboring cities were usually bittersweet, infused with longing. They told tales of ocean journeys and mythological figures. This song must be the latest fashion from Nalim Ima, like epaulets, but it sounded so contrary to everything she had heard of Kalan Jherin and his palace. He was a powerful sorcerer, with his black-wing flag and his tracts about the souls of Fanarlem. Surely he wasn't stomping to Su-za-na?

With the men now so merry, Lieutenant Dlara began another song. A stranger tried to grab Velsa's hand. She darted back and Grau stepped between her and the other man.

"Don't keep her to yourself, Thanneau!" He was a pretty fellow with big brown eyes and a light tone, but she didn't dare trust anyone who grabbed her hand.

"Velsa's shy."

"It's just a dance! Nobody's going to hurt her. But come

on, have a little pity, they don't let any women in the camp."

Velsa felt the tension in Grau's arm, and she knew he wanted to say some retort to defend her.

Flower was watching her from the other side of the fire. The red and orange of the flames reflected in her glass eyes. She didn't seem to like the men who had watched Velsa dance, who wanted her attention now.

Well, that makes two of us.

"I'll dance with Rawly," she said, offering her hand to him, praying that this might ease the situation. "He's been very nice to me."

Rawly pretended to wipe a tear of joy. "This is the first time I've ever had luck with a woman for being nice."

The pretty fellow laughed and stepped back, and Grau laughed too, and she knew she'd managed the situation as far as they were concerned, but Flower was still glaring as Rawly spun her around to another song.

"You're kind of heavy," he said.

She frowned. "That's what Grau said. What do you all think I'm made out of? I'm sure I'm not any heavier than Flower."

"Well, I've never touched *Flower*," Rawly said. "She terrifies me. And Fanarlem girls aren't my type; I like a good fight too much."

"A good *fight?*"

"Yes. I don't know, I get excited when a woman yells at me —at least, if I think we'll make up in the end. I don't suppose you can fight with Grau. It certainly wouldn't be the same."

Grau said he wanted her as a wife. An equal. But they never had fought.

Only once had she even dared to question him.

The golden band around her neck weighed upon her. She had begged him to remove it and he wouldn't—he had reasons that sounded sensible, but she wondered if he would feel the same if he was the one with untrained telepathy. Would he voluntarily lock away his own ability? His own *senses?*

125

They had no privacy at the camp. Velsa lay awake in a room full of breathing men. Grau fidgeted, even in his sleep. She wondered if he was having bad dreams. She missed the tender solitude they had shared on their journeys, the gentle love-making that led to a blissful sleep. Six months of this? It seemed unbearable.

Over the next few days, Grau went through a succession of tests and training. The attitude at the camp everywhere seemed laissez-faire. Men loitered around the camp, their appearance so disheveled that it might have been a refuge for hobos. Squads went out on patrol every day, to return with no reports of interest. The hierarchy of the military seemed confused. They were supposed to be working for the nation of Atlantis, but Kalan Jherin was the name spoken of with the greatest respect.

Velsa was allowed to accompany Grau everywhere, but could only sit and watch him. Her childhood had often been just as dull, but her patience for boredom seemed to have fled with all the things she'd seen and done in recent months.

He was handsome with a sword in hand, or demonstrating his ability to start a fire with sorcery. She liked watching him in action. But she would have preferred to be useful herself.

In the evening, sometimes they stayed for the music. Velsa kept quiet, trying to avoid any notice from Flower, but the other concubine was always staring at her.

She and Grau took a walk around the camp on a morning of blue sky and bright brisk wind. Grau's hand was warm in hers. They talked of their future, their dreams growing more wild and improbable by the moment. They might both become great sorcerers together, they might buy their own land in the marsh and build a house with an orangerie and a huge library and a stable with two beautiful horses they would take riding through the grasses...

They turned a corner and Grau trailed off at the sight of one of the soldiers humping Flower against the wall. Velsa pulled Grau back, turning around the way they had come, but it was too late. Flower saw them with her glassy eyes. The sight of her there, her body small and limp and accepting, was seared on Velsa's mind.

Velsa's steps stumbled a little as they walked away.

Archel bought Flower for this purpose, she thought. *Once, she must have waited in a House, imploring the fates for a kind master the same way I did. And this is what she got.*

She had always been told that concubines were safe from a life of prostitution, that they served only one man, like an arranged marriage. One might worry over a cruel master, but at least there would only be one. She wondered why it had never occurred to her or any of the other girls that the man might want to sell her to others.

Maybe it had simply been too terrible a thought to ever consider.

CHAPTER ELEVEN

One afternoon during Grau's rifle training, Lieutenant Dlara approached her and said, "Sorcerer Thanneau told me you can read."

"Yes, sir."

"How about if you read some books from the base library, so you'll have useful knowledge? You could be our unofficial scholar."

Scholar? Lieutenant Dlara was actually giving her a *purpose*.

She feared that a reading Fanarlem would attract as much attention as an eating Fanarlem, and certainly she still attracted attention everywhere she went. But he had already provided her with an explanation, if anyone challenged her right to read books. "Thank you, sir. I'd be happy to."

He chaperoned her to the library, a small room which must be almost directly under their bedroom, which contained four shelves of books and some cabinets of documents. A few tables and chairs rested by the windows for study; they were empty at the moment. She was immediately drawn to a book titled *Fanarlem Life: History, Construction, and Upkeep*.

"So I know what to do if I break," she said, to explain.

"Of course."

She settled back in the field before opening her book.

Introduction to the Reader

It has been centuries since we unlocked the secret of artificial life, but this great magic remains frightening and mysterious to much of the populace. When faced with even the most lifelike of flesh-born Fanarlem, people struggle for words of pity or ask many questions. How did it happen? How do you survive?

Since childhood I have been stricken with a malady that has defied the efforts of healers and sapped the magic from my blood, so that by the age of twenty-seven, despite a promising career, I found myself struggling through my days, forced to rest after taking even short walks. I was warned I would be confined to my bed within a few more years, with death soon to follow, unless steps were taken.

As the only child of a widowed mother, death was unacceptable to my soul and familial duty. The commonly accepted path was to visit a necromancer who could transition my body into an undead state—bearing in mind the many ramifications; the body that could no longer heal itself, but would be ever-dependent on sorcery.

Undead, I would largely preserve my outward appearance and my ability to move throughout society without attracting stares of pity or misguided condescension from everyone I met.

Still, I was intrigued by the second option. The Fanarlem body, which strips away most nuisances of human need entirely and for which many repairs could be accomplished by myself or any local craftsman. Why should we, the creators of this great magic, leave it only for slaves and not for ourselves?

Against the urgings of my friends to be sensible and even my mother's tears, I chose the life of a flesh-born Fanarlem ten years ago. I have adapted to its surprising advantages and disadvantages, learned the nuances of construction incorporating the newest techniques and materials, and have educated countless strangers about the truth of my existence, which is not worthy of anyone's pity.

And if you yourself are faced with the choice between death, undeath, and artificial life, or if your soul currently dwells in an artificial house and you are struggling to find acceptance, I hope this book will bring you to greater comfort and understanding.

Humbly Yours,
I. H. Orhan

Velsa had not expected the book to be written by an actual Fanarlem. A flesh-born Fanarlem—what Grau hoped to pose her as. Maybe this book would tell her how to pretend she had gone through such a transition.

She was so fascinated by the book that she could hardly tear her eyes from it. She had never read anything about her own kind that didn't dwell strictly on how Fanarlem were cursed and what they had to do to purify their karma. This book spoke to her directly as if she was going to make her own body and repair herself.

She heard soft footsteps coming up behind her.

It was the first time she'd seen Flower during the day, before dinner. The other concubine was still wearing her fine silk robes, and carefully sat down on the dry grass beside Velsa.

Velsa shut the book.

"What are you reading?" Flower asked, touching the cover as if to see it better.

But Velsa didn't think she could read. Her eyes never moved with any comprehension.

"A book on Fanarlem construction," she said, a little reluctantly. "Lieutenant Dlara said I ought to be informed."

"Why would *you* need to know that?"

"Well...if I need repairs, I can do them, or tell Grau..."

"Grau can't take you to a proper shop?" Flower scoffed. "He can't really afford you, can he? What will you do when your bones crack and your skin frays? That's why you never show any of your precious skin, isn't it?"

Anger briefly flared in Velsa's heart, but mostly, she still just felt pity for Flower, who had so much attention but little else. Velsa could only see one of the girls she had grown up with, the fear in her eyes twisted to cruelty as more and more of those fears came true.

Flower snatched the book from Velsa's hands and started running.

"Hey!" Velsa cried, her reverie of pity cut short. Grau was across the field; she couldn't tell if he'd even heard her yell.

Velsa ran after Flower. More than anything, she was terrified that Flower would destroy the book and Velsa would never know what it said. It seemed unlikely that the book would be replaced.

Flower's robe fluttered ahead. She ran faster than a Fanarlem should run. Velsa's joints creaked; she felt the impact of her footsteps rattling up her whole frame. *This is what she wants; she's hoping I'll break.*

Velsa stopped before the field was out of sight entirely, reluctant to move beyond where Grau could find her. "Please!" she cried.

Flower stopped too, just out of reach. They stood on the edge of the tenting grounds. A few of the rougher men who slept in the tents were milling around, and quickly gathering into an audience. She dangled the book over the nearest campfire.

"I don't want to get in your way," Velsa said. "I'd be your friend if you let me. I know you're mistreated—"

Flower shoved the book into the fire, underneath a simmering pot of beans.

"Oh no..." Velsa ran forward.

Flower laughed. She knew how carefully Velsa avoided the fire at night. Low flames lapped at the book's cover.

Velsa grabbed the book and flung it on the ground, stomping on the spot where smoke trailed upward. She glanced at her hands, finding only a few smudges of ash. Her hands hadn't gone up in a burst of flame like she'd feared.

Flower shoved her.

Some of the men whooped with excitement. "There you go, Flower!" one of them said. "Somebody ought to show her who's boss!"

Velsa stumbled, her boot hitting the charred logs on the fire's edge. Flower kicked her other foot, knocking Velsa off balance. She hit the ground and Flower flew on top of her, holding her down.

Grau and Rawly were right—Fanarlem girls *were* heavy, at least, if you didn't expect the weight. Flower's hair tickled Velsa's

131

cheek. "Fanarlem don't *read*," Flower snarled in her ear. "It's forbidden."

"No, it isn't! They taught me at my House and I'm sure they wouldn't have if—"

One of the men picked the book up from the ground. "*Fanarlem Life!*" he said. "Who needs a book on that? Do what we say, that's Fanarlem life." Chuckling, he moved to drop it in the fire again.

Velsa lashed out, hardly knowing what she was doing. She had saved Fern once—the power was there if she could dig it out. This time, she felt a wisp of control—of her own bending will, shoving past the golden band. Heat flashed in her temples, and her eyes filled with stars.

The man clutched his head with a cry of surprise. The book fell, undamaged, back on the dirty ground. "What in curses? That little wench used magic on me!"

The gathered men murmured with concern.

"Grau taught her magic," one of them said, and it seemed like a threat.

They didn't seem to realize it was telepathy.

Velsa was on the brink of ruining everything for Grau as well as herself.

Flower caught one of Velsa's hands and shoved it into the smoldering ashes. The man Velsa had attacked eagerly joined her, grabbing Velsa's other hand, pressing her skin against one of the flaming logs.

Velsa screamed. The stories she had once read, of wicked Fanarlem burning to death, had not lied about the pain. She didn't want to show weakness but she couldn't help the cry that broke from her lips. "Grau! Grau, *please*, help!"

"Can't handle a little pain?" Flower hissed. "I imagine not. Grau doesn't discipline you at all."

The man grabbed the back of Velsa's collar and yanked her back from the fire. "If you want that pretty sorcerer of yours to keep you safe, you'd better not give us anything to complain about."

"Please," Velsa said. "Lieutenant Dlara told me I could read—that I *should* read, to make myself useful."

"I think Dlara's a Fanarlem-lover," the man hissed.

"I think someone needs to teach you a lesson," Flower added.

"Velsa!" Grau's shout was so loud it seemed to bounce off of the ground. "Let—her—*go*."

The man threw Velsa to the ground and rose to challenge Grau. Grau's sword was drawn, but he didn't use the sword nor magic—he came straight in with a fist striking the man's face. "Don't touch her," he snapped.

"Oh, not so soft for once?" the man said, rubbing his cheek. "Usually I think you're wrapped around your whore's finger. Did anyone ever tell you it's supposed to be the other way around?"

"Velsa is mine." Grau pointed his sword at the man's neck. "I'll treat her how I like and it isn't your business. Some men don't get their kicks from abusing women, and if that makes me soft, I'll take it."

"You can't abuse a Fanarlem," the man said. "That's your problem, there—forgetting that she's cursed."

Grau bared his teeth; she knew he was unable to retort without admitting that he didn't believe this.

"How about dropping the weapon and I'll test you man to man?" his opponent suggested. "No swords, no magic, and no pot shots."

Grau handed his sword to Velsa. It was almost too heavy for her to hold.

The other man, who was not wearing his uniform jacket but just the shirt beneath, rolled up his sleeves. Some of the gathered crowd started chanting, "Fight! Fight!" Flower's fingers were laced, her expression excited. Velsa glanced at her own hands, damaged by the fire. Her skin was blackened, with a few puffs of stuffing poking out from charred fingers, but the pain had vanished the moment her hands no longer made contact with the heat.

Grau and the other man circled a few paces, their eyes locked on one another. The crowd kept edging back to give them more room. Half the camp must have been here by now. The smell of burning beans was in the air as the campfire was completely ignored.

Grau made the first move, lunging at his opponent—but as the other man drew back and lifted his arms to block, Grau darted back a step and then tried to surprise with a kick. The other man dodged this, too, and tried to take advantage of the moment Grau withdrew his leg, throwing a punch that Grau tried to evade. The fist knocked against his cheek, but not hard.

Velsa tried to remind herself of the Ten Thousand Man Sacrifice, and Grau's magical blood. He couldn't really be hurt. Still, she cringed back as the other man followed his punch with an uppercut, and this time he struck Grau in the jaw.

Grau quickly tilted his head back and forth, shaking off the pain, and lunged at his opponent, almost knocking him into the fire. Now they were on the ground and Grau had the upper hand, getting in a few good, fierce blows so the man's nose and forehead were bleeding—but then the man shoved him off. They rolled in the dirt. It was all happening so fast now, and turning into a wrestling match.

"What in curses is going *on* here?"

Lieutenant Dlara had arrived on the scene.

"Sorcerer Thanneau!" Lieutenant Dlara snapped.

Grau got to his feet, snatching up the hat that had fallen off his head and brushing dirt from his uniform. "Sir," he said, but his tone was not apologetic.

The other man got to his feet more lazily, almost grinning. "Lieutenant Dlara," he said. "I guess I got carried away."

The gathered crowd, which had been eagerly chanting moments ago, were now attempting to look concerned and confused, like they had all just shown up that second.

"They burned Velsa's hands," Grau said, taking his sword back. He tried to put a hand on Velsa's shoulder, but before she would let him, she took the opportunity to pick her book up out of the dirt and clutch it close.

"Velsa should not be reading that book," Flower said, drawing herself up like a noble lady. "She shouldn't know how to read at all."

"I let her take it from the library," Lieutenant Dlara said. "She's just sitting around most of the time, so I wanted her to study information that may come in handy."

"I was always taught that reading leads to willful thoughts," Flower said, "and it seems to me that Velsa has enough of those already."

"*Velsa* has willful thoughts? Who is arguing with an officer?" Dlara barked at her.

Flower dropped her eyes to the ground. "I am sorry, sir."

"If I tell Velsa she may read, that's the end of the matter," Dlara said.

Another one of the officers approached, a man named Kellen who always welcomed Flower's attentions at dinner.

"What's going on?" he asked. "Is everything all right?"

Flower started to cry, lowering her head and turning her toes together a little so she seemed younger, more fragile. "I didn't mean to upset you, Lieutenant Dlara, sir, it's just that I can't read and I was always told that Lord Jherin doesn't approve of Fanarlem girls who can read. I thought it was sinful. I thought it was my duty to burn Velsa's book because that's what I've always been *told*. I didn't know it belonged to the library."

Lieutenant Dlara sighed loudly as Kellen went to comfort Flower.

"I'm not so sure Velsa should be reading," Kellen said.

"She has a brain," Dlara said. "It's utterly pointless for her to sit around staring at the grass all day when she could be learning about medicine or tracking or useful plants, or in this instance, her own construction so she may be able to repair her injuries. There is no law against a Fanarlem reading."

"I'm not so sure," Kellen repeated.

"I am extremely sure, because I studied law before I came here and I had a class devoted entirely to the rights of slaves,"

Dlara said. "And in fact, you know perfectly well this is true because we've hired Fanarlem slaves to record documents for us. Velsa and Flower can do anything their masters permit, besides owning property, voting, and matters of that nature. She can read all the books she likes, and in fact, I am inclined to think Kalan Jherin would approve. He encourages literacy and a Fanarlem who can read will surely have a better understanding of their place in the world."

"This one sure doesn't seem to understand her place in the world," said the man who had fought Grau.

"She could occupy her time in other ways that would be equally useful," Kellen said. "Mending uniforms, for example."

"Do I need to remind you all that Velsa is reading on *my* order? We are sorely lacking in education around here." Dlara gave Velsa and Grau a serious look. "Sorcerer Thanneau, you're dismissed. Take Velsa to the barracks and see to her hands."

"Yes, sir, thank you," Grau said.

The skin of Velsa's hands was ruined. Some of her fingertips had crumbled away, and a few of her fingernails had broken off. The fire must have burned off the spells that gave her skin more of a soft, human quality because now her palm wrinkled in a weird way when she flexed her fingers, which she kept doing, because she was ever so slightly fascinated by her own deconstruction.

"What should I do for your hands?" Grau asked.

"I'm sorry," she'll said. "I'll need new skin. And it will cost a bit because of the spells… Where is the repair kit Dalarsha gave you when you bought me?"

He dug out the bag under his bed and found the smaller bag within. She found the seam ripper and cut the stitches at her wrists, pulling skin and stuffing off her skeleton until nothing remained but polished wood and tiny screws. She flexed her finger bones.

"They work?" Grau said. "Without skin?"

"Sort of. I can move, but if I touch something…" She

rapped her fingertips together. "It doesn't feel like much."

"I didn't think you could move without skin. I thought that's why Fanarlem can't move when they're wet."

"Well, we can move a little, but imagine trying to move if your muscles were suddenly replaced by sodden wool sweaters. My framework has motion on its own, but not much *strength*. Flower will probably make fun of my hands at dinner, too…"

"She'd better not. Your little skeleton hands are cute. But you should have let Flower go. It's just a book. What if she'd shoved your whole face into the fire?"

"But it's a book about me," she said. "About Fanarlem, I mean. It's written by a man who used to be flesh and blood, and I think it'll help me learn how to pretend I used to be real, someday."

"What a snake that girl is…" Grau paced angrily.

"I might be a snake too if I was treated that way."

"Obviously I see how he treats her," he said darkly. "But that can't be helped. It can't be helped just like everything else in the world." He sat down, his face darkened, and took one of her charred hands, but he was looking into the distance. Despite the cold day, his hair clung to his brow from sweat; his uniform was grubby from the fight.

"Some things can be helped," she said. "I wish Flower would let me help her. I would teach her how to read."

"Don't you dare," he said. "She'll only hurt you. I have to worry about you first. You understand, don't you? We have to be selfish just to survive."

Painfully, she did. Just like the Fanarlem slaves at his house…she felt like she should help them, but she didn't know how. She didn't even like them and she didn't like Flower either, but she *felt* for them. She thought of their eyes, in the middle of the night, the memory of their dead gaze like a spoon hollowing out her own insides. Not her stuffing, but her soul.

CHAPTER TWELVE

With Grau's training finished, he started joining Lieutenant Dlara's squad on patrol. Velsa was allowed with him, although she had to ride behind him to keep his hands unencumbered. It was for the best, she thought grimly. Her body could help to protect him from arrows, since they refused to give him any armor.

Within a week she found herself dreaming of arrows. Not *too* seriously, but it certainly would be exciting to see a single arrow fly into a tree, because the patrol proved just as dull as everyone had warned. They walked the same path every day, along the steep bank of the river, watching the Miralem nation on the other side. Every day, the same. Not only was each day the same, nearly every hour was the same, because the river offered almost no change of scenery. Rushing waters, rocky bluffs, barren trees. The skies whispered of winter. Occasionally, a Miralem village or stone guard tower offered a landmark.

"You look so bored," Grau said, lifting her onto the horse on a cold morning. His breath emerged in puffs.

"Because it's so boring."

"You know what else is boring?" he said. "The marshes."

"The marshes aren't boring. We went on canoe rides and picnics and looked for animals. But here we're stuck plodding along."

"Remember your crystal," he said. "This is our chance,

now, when it's quiet, to study the energies of this place. Even from the back of a horse, you can get a sense of the ground, the rocks—what minerals do they hold? The trees, the plants…it might be autumn now, and they are quieter than in the spring, but if you listen long enough, they'll start to tell you what they're about."

Velsa wished she had Grau's patience. She loved the sensation of activating the crystal and sensing all the life around her, but then her mind would wander. She couldn't seem to listen the way he did, holding his crystal in one hand for an hour at a time and staying very quiet.

Even when they stopped for lunch, Grau would poke around, gathering rocks and seeds and the skull of a small animal. She enjoyed doing this in the marshes, but she had grown restless here. Maybe she just couldn't relax with the other men around all day, and Flower waiting in the camp every night.

When they stopped for lunch, she watched Grau turn over a rock with his boot and stoop to examine what was beneath it, and could only think how handsome he was, and how she wanted to have a different life with him, building a house of their own.

Velsa had taken to playing cook. She didn't really know how, at first, but the men in the squad seemed to find it a lot more fun to teach her how to cook than to simply cook themselves. She flipped sausages and stirred onions and cabbage, singing Dlara's harmonica songs as she went, because they never seemed to leave her head. "City ladies sing this song, doo-da, doo-da…the palace walk is five miles long, oh de doo-da day…" And if she made the food, no one cared if she tasted it as she went.

One of the most difficult adjustments to the Fanarlem form is losing the need to eat, drink, or digest food. At first you might imagine this to be a positive. Most of us had a day when the coffers were low or the harvest poor, and the food supply is short. At other times, our days are so burdened that we resent taking time from our work to eat.

One of man's great satisfactions, nevertheless, is the enjoyment of a good meal after a day's labors, and the rejuvenating properties of a glass of wine or spirits.

The newly reborn Fanarlem is likely to experience a sense of having a tenuous hold on the physical world, now that one's body is no longer signaling these needs.

Spells are available that allow a Fanarlem to eat, by way of creating a passage in the throat that will make food vanish. But eating without saliva makes for a foreign and unpleasant experience, and one may find that without the sensation of food traveling down into a hungry stomach, all pleasure is lost.

Her book, which she read while the men were polishing off the meal, offered strong opinions on eating. Velsa wondered if this was true for every flesh-born Fanarlem. She had adored food from that first bite of pastry.

The dream of posing as a real woman and being treated as such seemed ludicrous sometimes. It was so much more than getting false papers. It meant pretending she had a family, and acting as if she expected to be treated like a real woman with rights. It meant never slipping up and mentioning the House or anything about her childhood.

"Always buried in that book," Rawly said, sitting down next to her and taking a swig from a canteen.

"I'm almost done."

"And have you learned anything about Fanarlem life? It seems to me you could write the book yourself."

"No, I don't really know anything." It was always fun to rile Rawly up so she said, "I learned how lifelike skin spells are made. Take the flesh from one freshly deceased Daramon or Miralem, boil it for an hour and then strain out the solids...boil until reduced for ten more hours..."

Rawly almost spat out his drink. "Just when I was starting to think you were attractive, Velsa, I find out you're made from corpse juice."

"Not just corpse juice. You didn't listen to the rest. The reduction is then added to a fresh pot of water with rose petals and birch bark and boiled down again. Just a small amount of this potion is needed, it says. You would never know if I didn't tell you. I don't feel corpse-y, do I?" She squeezed his arm. Rawly was the only person besides Grau she would dare to tease like this.

"I suppose not, but I have a rule to never touch a corpse, so I can't say for sure."

"Trying to steal her away?" Grau had come over to sit with them too. "I can't leave you two alone for a second."

"Nah, I prefer a really buxom girl." Rawly held up his hands like he was groping large breasts.

"Good luck with that," Grau said. "Sounds more like a Miralem than a Daramon."

"Well, maybe you don't get out enough, Grau. I have a girl at home just like that. Have you ever seen her?" Rawly took a tiny painting in a frame from his pocket, of a girl with curly hair, large breasts pushed up above the edge of her waist sash, and an awkwardly proportioned face.

"Are her eyes like that in real life?" Grau asked.

"Like what?"

"One higher than the other."

Rawly squinted at the painting. "*No.* I painted it myself."

"You detailed her breasts very nicely," Grau said. "I can see where your focus was."

"What's she like?" Velsa asked. She was growing more curious about real women. She had only ever spent time with Preya and Grau's mother, and the House-mistresses, and none of them seemed much like her or each other.

"She's loads of fun," Rawly said. "You remind me of her a little, sometimes."

"Do I?" Velsa said, excited.

"Only when we're talking like this, though. You're very quiet in groups, which I guess is only proper, but it's too bad. Grau, did you know she's made from corpse juice?"

"Can't be much. She's not very juicy," Grau said. "Look what I found." He held up a shimmering blue thick sliver of something about the size of his palm.

"A crystal?" Rawly asked.

"No. A dragon scale."

"Really?" Velsa reached out to touch it. It had a comfortable weight, and a satisfying shape that could have been a small plate for holding bread at dinner. "Where was this?"

"In the grass." He looked up. "Maybe the rumors were right. A dragon did pass through here."

"You're making me nervous," Rawly said. "Patrol is boring but that doesn't mean I'd want dragons coming around!"

"It was dropped months ago," Grau said.

"Months? That isn't enough distance between me and a dragon."

"Hmm." Grau turned the scale over. "I think it's long gone," he said, but he sounded wistful.

Weeks passed, each day the same. She understood now why the men were happy to see Flower's flute performance every night, and why Dlara's harmonica brought such excitement, even though he only seemed to know five songs.

The longest day of the year brought celebration. The Daramons in the city usually celebrated Ancestor's Day with their families at this time, but the girls at the House of Perfumed Ribbons had never celebrated because they had no ancestors. No one had family at the camp either, but a wooden crate had arrived at the base, wrapped in red and black ribbons with the seal of the Wodrenarune.

The men clamored to see it opened. The camp had no room large enough for an assembly, so they stood out in the cold. Grau and Velsa were close to the front because of Grau's rank as a sorcerer. Two of the men gently pried open the top. Lieutenant Dlara lifted out a large painting of Kalan Jherin himself.

Everyone gasped.

The painting was utterly lifelike. The tiniest detail of Kalan Jherin's proud, beautiful face was so perfectly captured that it might be expected to speak. He wore his black winged headdress and a sharply pointed collar that framed the graceful shape of his cheeks. His expression was noble, his eyes looking off into the distance. Really, it was disturbing—almost like the real Kalan was trapped within the frame. He never seemed to look older, in all of his two hundred years—not in paintings, at least. She wondered how long a Daramon might live, if they could afford to have healers tending to every small sign of age.

Velsa kept thinking with a shudder of his *Treatise on Fanarlem*, but she couldn't deny that he looked like a great sorcerer should.

Next, they unwrapped a protective cloth from a curious object, a wooden box with a crank on the side and a large, beautifully painted purple horn mounted to it. A magical implement of some kind, no doubt. Velsa stood on her tiptoes to see.

Lieutenant Archel held up a letter with Kalan's seal and read it aloud. "'There is no greater strength among the Daramon race than our fighting men. I know how difficult it is to be far away from your families for months and years on end, and I hope you will take some joy this afternoon in this taste of the wonders of our clever people. Here in Nalim Ima, we have been developing all manner of devices that will change our world—and they don't rely on sorcery at all. They can be used by anyone. First, there is the 'pho-to-graph' which captures a picture of the world exactly as it looks to our eyes. I have had a photograph taken of myself to demonstrate to you all.'"

"That's what you need," Grau told Rawly, who stood near them. "Kalan's eyes are right on the level."

"You're a cruel man to knock another man's artistic skills, Thanneau," Rawly said.

"'There is also the 'pho-no-graph' which plays music over and over again, without wasting a single crystal'," Archel continued. "'They are already popular in Nalim Ima and soon will be all over the Daramon nations. The music is contained within cylinders, much like a singing crystal, to hold different songs. A cylinder is included with a song called a Cake Walk that I hope you will enjoy.'"

The room was tense with anticipation as the officers read the directions. They took the cylinder from a little paper box and mounted it at the base of the horn, and turned the crank.

After all of this, Velsa expected to hear the most glorious music of her life.

Instead, it was a strange tinny noise, like it came from far away.

"What *is* it?" Grau asked. "If these things don't work with magic, how *do* they work?"

"I don't know," she said. "Is it like a clock?"

"But even clocks are powered by magic crystals," Grau said.

"Some things work without magic, don't they?" she asked. "What about the wheel of a mill?"

"Hmm."

"Maybe we could look at it more closely later."

Lieutenant Dlara played the Cake Walk several times through, until many of the men began to wander back to their tents, some of them muttering that they'd expected the crate to hold something a lot better. Others had come closer to poke at it.

Later in the evening, Lieutenant Dlara permitted them to inspect it. The phonograph had been moved into the library. Velsa looked through the manual at the instructions for disassembling some of the parts while Grau ran his crystal over the horn and box. "It's true," he said. "No magic at all." He wound it up again. "No wonder it sounds so dead."

"I think it sounds a little better now, without so many people around, when we can really hear it. It reminds me of 'Oh Su-za-na' in a way." Velsa couldn't help pumping her hands up and down to the merry beat.

"Why would it be called a Cake Walk?"

"Maybe it's how you walk when you're excited to have cake." She offered him her hands. He laughed and marched her across the room.

"It lends itself to a very different sort of dance, doesn't it?"

he observed.

When the song finished she followed the instructions in the manual to turn the crank backward and release some sort of mechanism made of metal parts. They were unusually smooth and uniform, as if shaped by a sorcerer, but she didn't sense the slightest trace of magic clinging to them either, besides what remained from the material itself. The phonograph reminded her of the diagrams inside *Fanarlem Life* showing how to put a skeleton together.

"What is going on in Nalim Ima?" Grau asked. "Who is figuring out how to make this magic? It has to be magic. There's no way you could make music and pictures the same way you'd build a mill wheel."

"What about…a printing press?"

"Tell me how you could make music with a printing press! No, this must be some sort of magic that can't be sensed with a crystal or with regular sorcery. Some test he's sending out to military camps to see if we understand what it is, that will eventually lead to cloaking weapons of war."

"Maybe it really isn't magic, though," Velsa said. "Look at the label. The Victor Talking Machine. It's a machine. I really think so, though I have no idea how it works…" She couldn't imagine anyone would put so much specific detail into a mere test for a war weapon.

Grau scratched his head, sliding his hat sideways. "Maybe you're right. But it still doesn't make any sense and there's something about it that makes me uneasy."

"Why?"

"I don't know. It's the same feeling I had in my gut when I saw that the Marnow house was gone," he said. "Still, before we go, we can do that Cake Walk dance one more time."

CHAPTER THIRTEEN

Velsa remained fascinated by the Talking Machine. She dreamed of taking it apart and putting it back together again, to see if its mystery might be revealed. No one would permit the gift from Kalan Jherin to be disassembled, however, so she had to content herself with listening to the Cake Walk, inspecting all the phonograph's parts, and reading the manual over and over.

Certainly, besides the books, the phonograph was the most interesting thing around. The very nature of patrol life kept her close to Grau but far away at the same time. The only place they might be alone was in the washroom or the latrines. The washroom was just a thin door away from the beds, and thus not really private at all, and Velsa refused to make love inside a latrine.

Grau liked to tease her every evening by reminding her how much time they had left.

"Only four and half months to go," he said, as they climbed the stairs to their barracks after a pleasant evening around the fire.

"Four and a half months is an eternity."

"And then maybe we'll go buy ourselves a barn. Seems to be all we need."

She raised an eyebrow at him. "Do you not miss me at all?"

"Oh, I miss you. I'm just a very patient man. All good sorcerers must learn to be patient and controlled."

"Your father wouldn't approve of all this patience and control, wasting your money…"

"You're the one who wants privacy. I'd be willing to try finding some out of the way spot…"

"So we can run into Flower again? No, thank you." The wall where they had found Flower with the other soldier was certainly one of the most private spots, but Velsa had never even walked that way again.

He stopped in the hall and ran a hand through her hair. "You just need to concentrate on your magic lessons more and less on…" He trailed off as she slid her hands along his back, drawing him closer to her. "Just who is the concubine around here anyway?"

He kissed her, her back pressed against the wall, and she wrapped his arms around his neck. He lifted her legs so they were wrapped around him, his pelvis against hers, nudging her, stirring her desire. She had to shake off the bad memory of Flower in the same pose. It certainly felt nice when it was Grau.

The door swung open and Rawly whistled.

She dropped her feet to the floor.

"Can't anyone have a moment around here?" Grau said.

"Nah," Rawly said. "Sorry. I need to go use the can."

"Yeah, *right*," Grau said. "Why didn't you go before coming up here?"

Rawly threw up a hand and went to the stairs.

Velsa looked at Grau miserably. Even if they had a tent, all those bored soldiers who always milled around outside would probably come snooping if they heard any interesting noises or noticed any interesting silhouettes.

They climbed into their bed, and in a few more minutes it was lights out. Rawly returned, banging his foot on the bed frame in the dark. The usual sounds of snoring resumed.

Grau slid a hand between her legs, nudging aside the fabric of her chemise. "Shh," he whispered in her ear. "You don't have to breathe, so I think you can be very quiet, can't you?"

She spread her thighs, with the smallest sigh of relief, and pressed back against him. He hadn't touched her like this in weeks.

She *could* be quiet, but that didn't mean it was easy. His fingers moved in firm, deep strokes, and she chewed on her lip.

The bed creaked if she dared to move too much, and oh, he knew just how to tease her by now, how to coax her hips into movement. She wanted to help him but she didn't dare. Instead she pressed her buttocks against him, trying to stay still although she felt his own arousal, trembling against her.

His other hand moved to plump her breast, then pinch her nipple so the skin tightened. It always amazed her, how her body seemed to come alive when he touched her. This was what she yearned for, more than anything.

He nibbled her earlobe, sending a shiver all the way down her back to the spot where his right hand stroked faster.

She wanted so badly to moan, to say his name. She leaned her head back, drinking in the sensations washing over her in waves that came ever stronger. Her mouth lolled open and she wanted to kiss him but not at the expense of losing the tongue grazing the edge of her ear…

He drew his hands and mouth back all at once.

"What?" She turned over.

His dark eyes were just glints of mischief in the moonlight filtering through the curtains. "I'm making a better, more patient sorceress out of you."

"Oh, no. *No.*" She shoved his shoulders.

He pulled her on top of him, his hardness nudging her. The bed squeaked and one of the snores stopped.

She drew back, embarrassed. She had gotten caught up for a moment, but no, she was not about to make a spectacle of herself.

"Meet me in the hall…if you dare," Grau said. He climbed out of bed and crept out the door.

"You!" she hissed, wrapping the blanket around her body like a cloak. It sounded like everyone was awake now and someone laughed as her stocking feet rushed past them in the dark.

Grau was waiting outside the door and grabbed her, tightening the blanket around her. She was torn between laughter and protest when he slung her over his shoulder and carried her to the stairs, down to the flight between the floors.

"I think we have the stairwell to ourselves," he said.

"I hope it stays that way. Everyone heard us."

"I was kidding about patience." He held up the jar of oil. Usually that was tucked away in his bag, and she gave him a smug smile.

"You planned this little strategy, didn't you?"

"Sorcery is one thing. You are another thing."

The look in his eyes, hard and soft all at once, never failed to thrill her. It was difficult to believe, nowadays, that she had ever been afraid of him, even from the first time she saw those eyes. But her time at the House already seemed so long ago.

He dropped the waistband of his pants just enough to slick himself with the oil, scoop her up and push himself into her. She battled the blanket off of her arms so she could wrap them around him, finally letting out the moan that had built up from all of his earlier attempts to provoke her. She still found some tiny, cruel part of her mind wandering back to Flower. Flower had probably never felt like this, like she truly wanted the man inside her. It was hard to believe the same act could be so sweet or so abominable.

"My beautiful wife," Grau said.

"Oh…" She never tired of those words. "But not yet…"

"Soon," he said. "I can't wait to whisk you away from here…and find a place where we can be happy."

She was almost in tears from the joy of it all.

From downstairs came the sound of a terrific crash and several loud bangs. They both jumped, and she cried out from surprise and pain as she knocked her head against the wall.

They broke apart, quickly fixing their clothes back to decency and rushing down the stairs. Grau pulled his magic light from his pocket. Nothing was apparent from the bottom of the stairs, but then, it had sounded a little farther away than that. Like it came from the library.

The library had a door with a lock, but Velsa couldn't say for sure if anyone really locked it. Either way, it was wide open now, and Velsa quickened her steps, knowing what was kept inside the library, what would make such a sound when it fell.

The pieces of her beautiful phonograph were scattered all over the floor. The wooden case had busted, the mechanism broken apart, and the horn was cracked and dented. It looked as if someone had dropped it and then taken a hammer to the pieces, to be sure no repairs were possible.

Grau took one look at the damage and then he ran out, dashing around the dark, abandoned headquarters and opening the door to peer outside. Apparently the culprit was gone. He returned alone as Velsa picked up the metal emblem that identified the Victor Talking Machine. She turned it over and over in her hand, as if the emblem held the machine's soul and could be restored to a new body, the way her own soul was caught in her eyes.

"Why would anyone do this?" Grau said.

They heard doors open, and in another moment Lieutenant Dlara walked in. Somehow, adding a pajama-clad, bleary-eyed Lieutenant Dlara to the scene made it even worse. "What happened here!?"

"We don't know," Velsa said. "We heard it break…"

"But whoever did it was gone," Grau said.

"I certainly hope no one in this camp harbors disloyal thoughts toward Kalan Jherin," Dlara said. "Someone needs to answer for this." He picked up a dented piece of the horn. "Either they had a key to the library or they picked a lock. You saw no one?"

"It took us a second to get down here," Grau said.

Velsa felt hollow inside, as if a friend had died, and she couldn't yet accept it. She might never see a phonograph again. Fates only knew how much it had cost.

"Go back to bed," Dlara said. "I'm going to question the

night guards and talk to the other officers."

In the morning, the camp was subdued but abuzz with gossip. Word of the shattered phonograph had spread, but no one had been punished. Everyone assumed it was an act of rebellion against Kalan Jherin, and Velsa certainly could see why someone might want to rebel against the severe man in the portrait, with all of his tracts and pamphlets supposedly handed down by fate, and his strange machines.

Flower strolled by. "You must be so sad, Velsa. I know how much you loved that thing."

Velsa stiffened.

Grau put a hand on her shoulder.

"Oh dear, you don't think I did it, do you?" Flower clasped her hands. "Such a violent act."

"You…didn't, did you?" Velsa asked carefully.

Flower came close enough to whisper in Velsa's ear. "I did do it," she said. "And good luck proving it."

"I've never done anything to you!" Velsa couldn't hold back her anger. "And you take it out on the phonograph?"

"You're the only one who really cared about it."

"You know if anyone does find out you broke something so expensive that came from Kalan Jherin…" She faltered, since she wasn't entirely sure what would happen to a law-breaking concubine.

"Dozens of men will vouch for me," Flower said. "Don't poke a wasp's nest."

When she left, Grau said, "We should still tell Dlara. Even if he can't do anything about it, he ought to be aware."

Lieutenant Dlara seemed unsurprised when they informed him. "Frankly, I'd still rather it be Flower's petty jealousy than an anti-Kalanite among us," he said. "I could speak to Archel about it…"

Grau made a hesitant sound. "I worry this might only make things worse. But this *is* the second time Flower has targeted Velsa, and she's willing to destroy camp property. What might she plan next?"

"I understand the hesitation," Dlara said. "The trouble with Flower is that she's slept with half the men in the camp. Archel doesn't care about her, so how can we expect her to care about anyone else? Her behavior is completely unacceptable, but the men like having her around, for their own selfish reasons, and it would cause a fuss if we brought the hammer down upon her."

"How is a concubine regarded, by law?" Grau asked. "If she hurt Velsa, what recourse do we have?"

"Archel would have to compensate you for any physical damages," Dlara said. "Unfortunately, it wouldn't be considered a crime against a person..." He looked uncomfortable.

Grau made a low sigh of frustration, took off his hat and smashed it in his hand. "Damn."

"I don't think there's much we can do," Velsa said, reluctantly, but she felt so helpless. Flower would always win, it seemed.

When they came to dinner that night, Flower was sitting on a man's knee, her head bowed against him while he rubbed her back, as if consoling her. Archel and Dlara were being very quiet. The men were passing the wine around themselves instead of being served by Flower.

A bad feeling tickled its way up Velsa's spine. Other men were filing in to take their places at the table.

"Something wrong, doll?" one of them asked Flower.

She gave him a pitiful look and then glanced at Velsa, and when she turned Velsa realized her hands were missing.

"She is being punished," Archel said curtly.

Hours before, Dlara had agreed with them that he wouldn't say anything about Flower's deed. Velsa sensed the tension between the two Lieutenants and Flower. Maybe Archel had found out on his own and been angry.

Either way, Flower's glare made Velsa shudder.

The men served themselves, but Flower still floated around the table throughout dinner, acting like a little girl scolded for stealing a sweet. She pouted and held her arms close to her body, giving shy glances through her eyelashes until she had been thoroughly assured that she was still just as pretty as ever.

Velsa could never watch her without a sick fuzzy feeling rising inside her chest, a mix of pity and…

Utter fury.

Did Flower have to act so brazen? As if she enjoyed being treated like a pet and a possession? If she was going to be angry, she should at least take it out on the men who abused her, not Velsa. It made Velsa feel tainted by extension.

Of course…she can't take it out on them. Velsa understood this too well.

Grau approached Dlara after dinner. "What is going on?" he demanded in a whisper. "I thought we agreed that punishing Flower would only make things worse."

"We did, but Archel could tell I was angry. He asked me if Flower had broken the phonograph, and he insisted she be punished. I told him that Flower might retaliate at Velsa, but… Archel really doesn't care about the affairs of Fanarlem girls. Not yours or his own. He does care about his own standing, of course, and Flower is his responsibility. My hands are tied. It might be even worse if I reported this to my superiors. I believe Lord Jherin has already considered banning concubines from camp. He feels it's a barbaric custom."

"I think I agree with him," Grau said.

Dlara's brow furrowed and he looked at Velsa. "I didn't mean in your case."

"But I do," Grau said. "Velsa shouldn't be here, exposed to all of this behavior."

"I understand," Dlara said. "I've never believed we should abuse Fanarlem. Velsa seems every bit as sweet as my own sisters. I half forget she isn't a Daramon girl."

Dlara was being nice but none of it made Velsa feel any better. By the time they got back to the barracks she felt like someone was pinching her from the inside. She already knew it would be a sleepless night.

Grau stepped into the washroom and came out in his army-issue pajamas. He suppressed a yawn and sat down beside

153

her on the bed. "If Flower hurts you," he said, "we'll leave this place."

"But at that point she'll have hurt me already."

"Well, you're not as easy to hurt as the phonograph, which is left unattended."

"I'm worth less than the phonograph. I wasn't a gift from Kalan Jherin," she said, in a low tone, because as usual they weren't alone. Their roommates were also changing into pajamas, turning back covers, talking about the day—luckily, no one mentioned Flower.

"*No*," Grau said. "I don't want to hear another word like that. You're infinitely more valuable to me, and I don't think I'm the only one. All the men in our squad like your cooking and the sweet, absent-minded way you're always singing 'Oh Suzana'."

"I have to be sweet," she said. "I was told I could never let myself be angry or rebellious, that if I did, I would be cursed to live this life over and over. Sometimes I can feel anger bubbling up, and I don't know what would come out. I might not be very likable anymore."

He laughed. "Ridiculous. You think I wouldn't like you even if you were angry sometimes? The fights I've had with Preya! The same goes for you. Maybe it will take time for you to believe it, but it's true."

CHAPTER FOURTEEN

Velsa was beginning to get very tired of making potatoes and cabbage with cured sausage. Every day, the same. Well, sometimes they had carrots or beets. Either way, she didn't care to eat it anymore. She felt sorry for Grau, that he had to eat every day, no matter how unpleasant the fare. She dreamed of pastries.

At least she had a new book to read while she stirred the lunch. Two weeks after Ancestor's Day, a carriage had arrived at the camp with a load of holiday gifts. The men were astonished to see the packages arrive so quickly, and even more astonished to open so many lavish parcels. The camp flooded with new handkerchiefs, cologne and shaving kits, but most especially, books. Novels, freshly printed in Nalim Ima with color plates, many of them about bold adventurers and heroic tales of war. The most popular one was about a steam-powered ship like the one Preya mentioned—the men were passing that one around so avidly that Velsa figured she'd be lucky to see it in a month's time. In the dark nights it wasn't uncommon to see men tilting books toward the fire to read them, turning pages with gloved hands.

Flower seemed even more nasty since the books had become the talk of camp, but there was no helping that.

Today Velsa had a book called "Jane of the Moors". The men weren't so interested in it because it was a romance. Velsa had started it yesterday and found it very strange because it was written from Jane's own perspective as if she were a real person, but it was a novel. The cover declared it, as if she wasn't the first reader to be confused. Once Velsa got used to the style, she could hardly put it down. Jane lived in an orphanage where everything was terrible and it reminded Velsa of the House, except that the children were always dying. The story must have taken place before the Ten Thousand Man Sacrifice...unless Jane was a Miralem? Oddly, the book never mentioned her race.

The story took a very exciting turn as the men were eating, when Jane met a strange man out on the moor who turned out to be the master of the house. Velsa thought maybe moors and marshes were not so different and imagined this Rochester fellow looked like Grau, even though he was supposed to be ugly. She wondered why such a rich man would choose to be ugly and not have his face shape-shifted. He would probably explain sooner or later. Rochester talked a lot. Everyone in the book talked in very long passages.

A whizzing sound made Velsa look up just as an arrow struck one of the men in the back.

She had barely registered this before a slew of them followed.

The camp erupted in uproar. Men shoved their food dishes aside and scrambled for the weapons they had tossed aside in their complacency. Only Lieutenant Dlara seemed to have maintained readiness; he had his rifle in hand and was shouting for the men to take cover in the brush. "Help your comrades, but hurry!" A few of the men had taken a nasty hit and while they wouldn't die, one had passed out and another young man was on the ground screaming with pain—or maybe fear. An arrow jutted out of his stomach.

Velsa's brain snapped to life; she ran to the soldier in pain, drew the crystal pendant out from under her shirt and snatched up a dropped flask of water. She tried to project healing light to him. Water had healing properties.

His screaming died back into a whimper, and she urged him to his feet. He was shivering violently and almost knocked

156

her over into the snow with his stumbling. One of the other soldiers came over and took the man off Velsa's hands, half-dragging the young man to cover.

Grau took out his crystal, waving his hand in the direction of the arrows. The sounds of choking and sputtering came from the bushes and trees as he manipulated the air so their attackers couldn't breathe.

"Fire, quickly, while Grau has a hold on them!" Dlara called.

The soldiers fired a round of shots from the brush where they had positioned themselves. They had spaced out into two groups, their shots angled to avoid catching Grau and Velsa in the line of fire.

A body fell from one of the trees, while another cried out and staggered into the camp, collapsing on the ground.

Velsa had never seen death before. She had no time to consider it now. Grau was bent forward, one hand clutching his crystal, murmuring to himself. Velsa clutched her own crystal, but she had none of Grau's skill.

Something changed in the air, just then. Velsa felt a little sick.

A haze settled on her mind, blurring the edges of her vision, and robbing her desire to move.

Someone was in her head, a shapeless presence that smelled like burning hair and felt like a snake slithering up her rib cage. She stood in the center of the camp, trying to remember what she was supposed to be doing, as two dozen Miralem burst out of the bushes and dropped from trees. They were a grubby, colorful lot—obviously not soldiers. The bandits, most likely. Velsa's knees threatened to buckle. She managed to look over at Grau and saw him bending forward, a hand on his head, obviously struggling through the same feeling.

Their men had stopped firing. A few of them groaned or made odd sounds like they were trying to speak but could no longer remember how. She wasn't sure she remembered how to speak either. She wanted to call Grau's name and her mouth wouldn't even move.

The Miralem held bows with arrows at the ready, the front line of them advancing toward the men in the brush while the rest started searching the camp. They grabbed packs, a rifle someone had dropped, a different novel one of the men had brought, canteens and plates and cigarettes—anything they could carry.

One of them was looking at Velsa. A woman, with gray hair in long braids and layers of clothing topped by a embroidered apron. She rushed toward Velsa, holding out a hand.

Velsa swayed a little, trying to stumble toward Grau, trying to scream. The telepathic attack was fading off, but time still seemed strange, like the Miralem were moving faster than her. In a panic, she threw the book at the Miralem woman. That must be what she wanted. And maybe, as cheap as books were getting, Velsa could have another copy of Jane of the Moors someday.

The woman caught the book in one hand but she kept coming. She scooped Velsa up like a sack of potatoes and threw her over her shoulder.

Velsa might have been heavier than Grau and Rawly expected, but this woman looked like eighty pounds of potatoes wouldn't make her blink.

The fog on Velsa's mind lifted, but now she was captive. Velsa flailed, pushing on the woman's back, trying to wriggle or fight her way out of the strong grasp. The woman handed her off to one of the Miralem men, who was even stronger.

"Grau!" Velsa screamed. She could see him behind a cluster of bushes, struggling to stand straight.

"Velsa…!" he called back, shaking his head. "Velsa—I'm coming—as soon as I can!"

The man started running with Velsa in his arms.

"Miss, we're trying to save you," he snapped.

"I don't want to be saved!"

"I know that's what they tell you," the man said. "Believe me, it's for your own good."

"You're kidnapping me!" Velsa said. "I don't want to be

saved! This is my home!" He was rapidly carrying her away in the wrong direction, toward the river.

"Aren't you a concubine?"

"I was, but—"

"Does a man own you? In the eyes of the law?"

"Well—yes, but—"

"You deserve better than that," he said. "You deserve freedom."

Her mind swirled with fear and possibility. If her soul was a Miralem, and the Miralem lands would offer her freedom...what if she belonged there, after all?

But she had already spun so many dreams with Grau. The house they would have, the gardens and horses and long walks in the marsh. Even if they couldn't really have such a life, even if they could only have a cottage...she couldn't leave him.

The man stopped at the bluff that led down to the river, and she thought here he might have to put her down and she might have a chance to run...one chance. Except, Fanarlem simply couldn't run as fast as flesh and blood people, certainly not a tall and athletic man.

She had barely finished the thought before he began scaling the steep bluff with her still in his arms. His feet seemed to know the safest places to plant themselves, and here and there he stopped gripping her legs to grab a rock or a root. They were on the riverbank in seconds, the other Miralem following. Crude rafts, tethered to the bank, were quickly piled with a bounty of supplies and released from their moorings.

"*Velsa!*" Across the river, Grau plunged through the bushes at the top of the bluff.

The woman put a strong hand on Velsa's back and forced her to turn toward the Miralem lands, away from Grau. "I know it's hard at first, but he won't do you any favors."

"Please," Velsa said. "I mean it. I don't want to go. I don't want to fight you." She tried to duck away.

The woman caught her arm. "Foolish," she said. "I suppose you think you love your 'master'. He's all you've known.

You're scared to leave."

"Don't touch me." Velsa yanked her arm free and ran to the bluff.

Other soldiers appeared at the bluff, firing on the Miralem at the rafts. The old woman who had been gripping Velsa just moments ago dropped to the ground, a red stain blooming on her apron. The arms that had easily lifted Velsa were now limp and lifeless. But the Miralem were fighting back, too. They fired arrows and Velsa feared she heard Rawly scream.

She clung to the rocks a moment, feeling the weight of the crystal on her chest, praying that her friends were protected. Rawly was still screaming.

The Miralem at the river were on their rafts now, disappearing with their loot down the rushing waters. One raft still remained.

It was quieter now. She heard only soft groans and a few exchanged commands, and looked up the bluff. Grau held down a hand. "I think it might be over," he said. "Should I come down for you?"

"I think I can climb…" She stepped onto a rock, and from there, reached for one of the roots. She managed to scrabble up the wall high enough to catch his hand, and he pulled her up onto the bank.

"You're all right," he said, embracing her tight.

"*You're* all right," she replied. "But…Rawly…" An arrow had gotten him right in the knee. One man was dosing him with pain medicine while the other pulled the arrow out—but Velsa looked away before she saw this act completed.

"We have a few serious injuries," he said. "But we'll heal. We're Daramons."

"That's right!" exclaimed another soldier. "The Miralem hardly stand a chance anymore!"

Not so cocky, now…

The voice was in their heads again, and it followed the statement with a sudden brunt of pain. Velsa shrieked and grabbed Grau, but it was no use. The pain came from within her own body, and Grau could not soothe her anymore than she could soothe him. His eyes were squinted shut as he made a shuddering sound, trying to fight off the invasion.

The moment seemed to go on and on forever. The pain was so powerful, it became the only thing that existed in the world. She was screaming and men around her were screaming. Their scream was like one endless sound.

Velsa raged at it. Her fury came from the same place as the pain itself. The pain almost seemed to feed her. The golden band was hot around her neck, so hot it was burning, but she would fight past it if it was the last thing she did, because this *had* to stop, or she would die of the agony.

She felt something snap, and suddenly it was over. Completely over. It seemed like the men should have been spitting up blood, for how that felt, but everyone was fine.

Grau let go of Velsa and ran toward the trees, on a mission. The men followed behind him, except the ones tending to the injured. Grau thrust a hand out, and one of the trees shook out a woman as if she were a nut.

"The telepath," Grau said, but they all seemed taken aback to find a woman. Rifles pointed at her, but no one fired.

"If you dare breathe," Grau said, "we'll fire."

Lieutenant Dlara approached from the camp. "Did you get him?"

"It's a she," a man said.

"I surrender," the woman said. "Please…I didn't know you had a telepath among you."

"A telepath?" Dlara said. "We certainly do not."

"You must! No mere sorcery could have thrust that pain back at me. Some Halnari traitor, no doubt?"

Dlara looked at Velsa. He knew immediately.

"Show me your neck, Velsa," he said.

Velsa was trembling now. They were all looking at her and she couldn't imagine what the consequences would be. She unfastened the top clasp of her jacket, showing the edge of the golden band.

161

"Do you have the key with you, Sorcerer Thanneau?"

"Yes."

"Take it off of her."

Grau produced the small golden wand. He looked unsure, but he followed orders, walking up to Velsa and tapping the band with the tip of the wand. The band split, and he removed it from her neck.

A rush of warmth flooded Velsa's entire body. The air seemed to crackle with thoughts—a vague sense of fear and uncertainty that they all shared.

"Give it to me," Dlara said.

"No, no," the Miralem woman pleaded.

Dlara ignored her so completely that Velsa didn't think he had experienced any of the pain. The telepath must have directed it only at the group standing atop the bluff, sparing anyone in camp. He snapped it around her neck. "Now go," he said.

She had her fingers wrapped around the band, tugging on it as if it might break for her, but Velsa knew that once on, they were seamless and as strong as a diamond. The woman ran for the bluff, shouting curses.

"Now," Dlara said. "I need you all to realize that Velsa fought on our side today. If certain people back in the camp hear that she is telepathic, and certainly if this leaks back to the higher ups, she will be sent away. I do believe her presence has brightened our squad and I have no reason to believe she would hurt us. So if you value what she did for you, in any small measure, I hope you will all keep your mouths shut. I know we have a golden band back at camp, so I'll restore hers when we return."

At his last words, Velsa almost sniffed back a sob.

For a moment, she thought she was free, but of course—Grau was right. Having her telepathy unbound in the camp was risky.

Feeling the warm power flowing through her body like blood, she thought she might die if a new band closed around her neck.

Maybe I should have chosen freedom, after all...

The men were solemn now, gathering the Miralem bodies and making a grave. Grau helped speed up the process by moving the earth. He received compliments from everyone for his skill at manipulating the elements.

No one thanked her at all. They looked at her as if she might turn on them at any moment.

Only when they were riding home, and she could hide her face in Grau's back, did the small sobs come. They forced their way out of her, no matter how hard she tried to restrain them.

Grau reached behind him, found her hand, and pulled it against his heart.

"Your skin is warmer," he said.

"I felt—warm—when the band—"

"I'm so sorry," he said. "I just don't know what else to do."

She understood this went beyond his own fears. And she understood those fears, too. Her powers were not controlled.

It still felt unbearable.

"Can you feel my thoughts now?" he asked softly.

"I feel that you're scared, a little bit. But I don't know whether you're scared of me, or of Miralem, or other soldiers finding out back at camp and sending me away. It's faint."

"All of the above, maybe," he said. "With an extra dose of awareness that we shot Miralem dead. I didn't do it with my own hands, but I was certainly a part of it all. They might be bandits, we might be considering war, but...well, it isn't easy to watch."

"No..."

He kept ahold of her hand as they rode back. When they returned, the sight of injured men brought everyone running. For those who hadn't dealt with the killing and the pain, this was simply the most exciting story they might hear in months.

Dlara immediately led Grau and Velsa back to headquarters. Velsa sat stiffly while he brought out the new band.

"I'm sorry," Dlara said. "I know they aren't pleasant to wear. But we couldn't permit you to be here without it. I have to act for the safety of everyone. Including you. And we do know, if

163

you are really in danger, you're able to tap into your powers. If I went by the book, I couldn't allow you to be here at all."

"I understand," she said curtly.

Dlara handed the band to Grau, but he passed it to her, as if he thought she might prefer to do it herself.

"No," she said. "You do it. I can't make my own hands do this to myself."

He hesitated. Dlara watched them patiently and kindly like a doctor delivering bad news. Velsa felt the faint new warmth in her own hands, warmth that came from her own power and not from Grau.

Grau lifted her hair and locked the band around her neck, choking off the warmth.

She clenched her fists. In this moment, she hated Dlara and Grau both. She should have gone with the Miralem. Surely someone in the Miralem lands could break the band's magic.

She should have chosen her freedom.

"Velsa...," Grau said.

She got up and walked to the door. She had to walk or she would yell at him. She'd tell him every dark thought she had ever harbored against him, and he would hate her; yes, he would, even if he said he wouldn't. No Fanarlem was supposed to have these feelings.

"Velsa!" He followed her. "Please understand—"

"No! No, no, I'll never understand. Don't touch me right now."

"I've been told to fear Miralem all my life—"

"And what else have you been told? What were you told about me, about my people? I'm not a Miralem, anyway, I'm a Fanarlem. I'm a Fanarlem who ought to be emotionless, and submissive. That's what you wanted, isn't it? It must be, because it's what you were told you'd be getting, and instead you got *me*."

"I don't know what you really want me to say. I was young and stupid and I feel like I've aged ten years since I met you. I've already told you I wasn't sure I'd buy a girl that night. I didn't really know what I'd find. I wanted magic and I found a real woman, and I've never regretted it, even when it's hard—but it *is* hard. It's hard because I love you, and I have to endure all the things people say and do to you, and half the time there's nothing I can do about it. But I know it's even worse for you, many times worse. I do everything I can to make you—"

"*Happy?*" She clutched her head, trying to stop herself. She sounded so angry—was that even her own voice?

She couldn't stop. These words had been building up for so long. But she tried to calm herself, just a shred. "You chose me knowing I was telepathic, and I hoped against hope that one day you would set me free. Those Miralem today offered me freedom, and I stayed because of you, but…that old woman said I was a fool, and she was probably right. I love you, Grau, but I hate this world…and sometimes I even hate you."

He looked struck, before snapping back, "Why?"

"Because of this!" She tapped the band. "Because you want a wife. But not an equal. Before we made love, you said you had been waiting for the day when I would be yours. You still see me as your possession, like all the rest, it's just that you're patient."

He looked past her. "And you wonder why I don't want you reading my mind." He sighed. "I was so enthralled by you from the start. And everyone *tells* me to treat you that way. Everyone else tells me you're a tainted soul, even Kalan Jherin, the man I used to believe spoke to fate itself, and it's only my gut and the look in your eyes arguing the other way. It's a wonder I don't question it more often, but your eyes are the most powerful force in my universe."

She met his eyes, then, and she could have said the same to him.

"Velsa, I wouldn't have bought you if I didn't see the way you looked at me—like you wanted to belong to me."

He took her hand, then he reached in his pocket for the small golden wand that locked her band. "I belong to you the same way. If you had gone with the Miralem you would have crushed my heart. I would have done anything to get you back. And if I had known you left of your own will, because you couldn't bear that I locked your powers away...I would have to give you this." He closed her hand around the wand.

"I can't take off the band," he said. "You know the men will be watching you now. But at least I can give you the key to your own prison."

She held the key a moment. The key, that had bound her all her life. At the House, she never even knew where it was kept.

She threw her arms around him, flooded with relief. "Thank you, Grau."

"Now, shall we join the others outside? I bet Rawly could use some cheering up."

"First, let me make an internal pocket to keep this. It's too important to lose."

"You mean, inside of you?"

"That's right. I'm useful that way." In the room, she searched the Fanarlem repair kit and found a scrap of fabric just large enough to hold the wand. The entire headquarters was so empty, she dared to slide her pants down a bit. She cut a few of the stitches that held her leg to her torso, around the same place a pants pocket would fall, just wide enough to nest the pocket under some of her stuffing. "See, now if I need the wand, I can reach under my jacket like I'm getting something out of my pants pocket, but it'll really be inside my leg."

"This is good to know. We might have to make you a few more pockets."

"Just not too many or I'll be full of little holes."

"But I could sew secret objects up inside of you..." He looked intrigued.

"Nothing too heavy! But yes. You could. I read a story once about a Fanarlem girl whose rib cage contained a magical goblet that her creator hid inside her."

"I'll have to think more deeply on this development later."

She rubbed his leg with her foot. "Does my storage capacity turn you on?"

"Well...maybe not put like *that*..."

166

The camp was bright with bonfires and some of the men were already singing of victory when Grau and Velsa joined them. Flagons lifted to Grau. "There he is! We were just talking about you, Thanneau. Tell 'em how you found that telepath in the tree!"

"Simple, really. If you talk to trees, they talk back. It just takes time. I've been talking to them for weeks already, so they know me."

"Like taming an animal," someone observed.

"I wouldn't say you can ever really tame a forest," Grau said. He drank some of the wine that was offered, and asked after Rawly.

"Here!" Rawly waved from a chair, his knee bandaged.

"Feeling better?"

"A good dose of healing potion works wonders." He reached for Velsa's fingers and gave them a kiss. "Thank you for your services today," he said under his breath.

She couldn't help a smile. "I'm glad I was able to do it."

"We have to make sure you get home safely to your girl with the large breasts and crooked eyes," Grau said.

"Oh, stuff it with that already."

Dlara joined them shortly for some harmonica music, and Grau whirled her around in a dance. No one else even tried to ask her for a dance now. She wondered if someone in their squad had whispered to others that she was telepathic. Even Flower wasn't glaring at her tonight.

The men in Grau's squad gossiped about the Miralem: "Did you see how old some of them looked? Why don't they shape-shift those wrinkles? It'd be nothing for them, and they don't do it." "Seems a shame that a few of them got taken out just for trying to steal a few rifles and books." "But I've heard that stuff can fetch gobs of gold at their markets. They're dying for Lord Jherin's treasures." "How times have changed! Must really sting to know they're not the chosen people anymore."

They might not have so much to boast about if I hadn't been there, Velsa thought. *But they'll never admit that a Fanarlem concubine saved their lives...*

167

Grau suddenly sat down, looking a little green. He must have been drinking more than she realized.

"Are you okay?" she asked. "Should we go back to the room?"

"Maybe...head's spinning."

"How much did you drink?"

He made a noncommittal noise. "People kept handing me more..."

She helped him up, but her body couldn't really support his staggering weight. "Come on," she said sternly. "It's not far but you have to keep it together."

It seemed to be hitting him so fast. She wondered if someone had given him harder stuff and he hadn't realized. He probably had some remedy for this in his bag, if she could just get him to bed. They made their way around the celebrating men, and Grau stumbled through the grass. When they reached the main building, he leaned forward and vomited on the ground.

She jumped back, quite disgusted.

He slid to the floor, barely conscious now. This was so unlike him. The men were always drinking in the evenings and he rarely had more than a glass. Even at the dance when he and Preya both seemed to want to dull their sense in drink, he had kept his head.

"Grau?" She put a hand on his shoulder. "Stay with me. Did someone poison you?"

"Hmm..." His usual 'hmm' sounded dazed rather than thoughtful.

"Wait here, then. I'll get healing potion."

She ran to the door and headed for the stairs, but no sooner had she stepped into the stairwell than one of the guards grabbed her. He'd been waiting in the stairwell. She was so surprised that he had already pulled her hands behind her back and cuffed them before she realized what had happened.

"A telepath, huh?" He lifted her over his shoulder, holding her legs so she couldn't kick. Her arms were useless trapped behind her.

168

When he walked her back out into the hall, Flower stepped out of the shadows.

"Darling, I've got her," the guard said.

"Velsa," she said. "The unsung hero of the day, so I hear. I'd better not take any chances. Flip her onto her back."

The guard grabbed Velsa's hair and pulled her back down into his arms. She tried to reach for her power as Flower approached. She couldn't seem to fight past the band at will.

As the guard held her head rigid with his tight grip on her hair, Flower kept Velsa's eyes forced open as she dropped liquid into them. A potion, of some kind. Because a Fanarlem's soul was held in their eyes, it was the only spot they could be affected by potions.

The ceiling seemed to dance above her. Velsa shut her eyes. "Did you slip this to Grau…?"

"Of course, my dear," Flower said. "Now, I certainly do wish I had time to sew your mouth shut. I've dreamed of sewing up that little mouth. But we'd better get moving. Potions don't work for long on Fanarlem." She tied a gag around Velsa's mouth. The gag had been made with obvious forethought—a wad of cloth was sewn to the inside, stuffing her mouth but she was unable to swallow it away with the vanishing spell. Any sounds she tried to make were very muffled. And then Flower tied a blindfold around her eyes.

Flower led the way, showing the guard out a side door. Velsa struggled to maintain awareness. The bouncing motion of her body as the guard ran with her in his arms was making her feel sick, as if she had a stomach full of wine herself. Her stuffing seemed to have a mind of its own, swishing around inside her. Of course, this had to be an illusion—that potion couldn't affect her stuffing—but it certainly felt real. She shut her eyes, trying to muster control, but it was almost impossible between the hands twisted painfully behind her, the mouth full of cloth, and the potion swirling through her thoughts.

Velsa didn't know what was happening. They kept walking quickly, for quite a ways. She heard the music still in the distance.

Where were they taking her?

Fight! she told herself. *Please—fight!*

She knew something horrid was about to happen, and if she didn't fight now, she couldn't stop it. But they had thought of everything; drugged Grau, drugged her, bound and gagged her, and they even knew that Dlara was busy playing harmonica and Rawly's leg was still recovering. Everyone who had ever been her ally was unlikely to notice in time that she was gone.

The guard stopped, and shifted her position to fumble with something. She heard the gates creak open.

They were going outside of the camp.

The music grew ever more distant. The night air seemed colder. Through the blindfold, she saw a light nearby—Flower must have had a light crystal.

"How I've dreamed of getting rid of you," Flower said. "From the day you arrived, a pampered princess. Grau doesn't want you to serve him, he doesn't want you to serve anyone. I'll bet he even holds you in the night, so tenderly. He probably tells you he loves you. You must have thanked every star in the sky the day he bought you...didn't you?"

Velsa moaned a plead. If she could just *talk* to Flower—

"You'll never see him again," Flower said. "I hope you know how to ascend."

Ascension—a death some Fanarlem chose for themselves, since it was very difficult for them to commit suicide—surrendering their bodies and releasing their own souls to their next life by sheer force of will.

What are you doing to me?

They wouldn't dare separate the eye that held her soul from her body. That would set her telepathic powers free as well. They must mean to lose her body in the woods. Maybe strip off her limbs so she couldn't move. Or else—

She heard the waters of the river, rushing in the distance, and suddenly she knew what they would do.

The water would immobilize her limbs. The current would carry her away. And the band would lock her from calling for help. She had the key, but she couldn't reach it. She tried to struggle, tried to cry out.

"Have you guessed your fate?" Flower said. "Hurry," she told the guard.

He ran faster, the rushing waters growing closer, until he was at the bank. He threw her over his shoulder again and scaled the bluff. Flower followed more slowly; Velsa could hear her making small sounds of struggle and dropping down hard, like she had half-fallen.

The guard threw her body down on a cold rock. He held her down, one strong arm on her chest, and the other pinning one leg, while Flower caught the other, but Flower was not so strong. Velsa kicked and it felt like her boot made contact with Flower's chest.

"If you struggle, Dar will bash in your rib cage," Flower said, her tone dripping with false sweetness, with loathing.

The fight drained out of Velsa. No, she couldn't attack them physically. She had to tap into her other powers.

She felt her crystal. She brought her sensations to life—the deep, ageless strength of the rock beneath her. How could she use the rock to fight? She didn't know how to move rock the way Grau moved dirt. Moving rock took great skill, he had told her. The rock might give her more power, more resilience, but she would still have to overcome a man who was trained in fighting.

Flower was unbuttoning her boots, exposing Velsa's toes to the air. "How old are you, Velsa? A grown woman, aren't you? And Grau couldn't be more than twenty-five. I don't think he's owned you long at all. Do you know how old I was when I went up for sale?" she asked. "Twelve. Twelve, and given the body of a woman. I was an innocent. I knew nothing at all, and I was there for a week when Archel bought me. He didn't know I was twelve, of course, I was told to lie. But then, I don't know if he would have cared anyway. What do you think that first night was like?"

Velsa wondered what the guard thought of all this. He must already know her story, since he didn't seem surprised.

She pulled off Velsa's trousers, peeled her stockings away.

"I was utterly helpless," she said. "Surely he must have washed away all my sins, that very night. I wish you could know how that felt. You would be so grateful to know you were cleansed."

Velsa grunted urgently.

Flower unfastened the clasps of her tunic, and made a small gasp when she saw the crystal. "Oh—look at this! An unexpected treasure." She unfastened the clasp, and all the crystal's power slipped from Velsa's grasp. Grau's gift to her, that she had chosen because it sang to her.

Sibalora! Listen to me!

Flower gasped. "Don't call me that name."

It is your name. You deserve a real name. I don't want to be your enemy. The Miralem bandits tried to kidnap me so they could give me freedom. They wanted to help me. Fanarlem are free in Miralem lands. Go across the river. Leave Archel forever. Save yourself—find a new life!

Flower slapped her face. "Shut up!"

"Is she talking to you?" the guard asked. "With her mind?"

"Get rid of her," Flower said. "Get rid of her now."

"Are you sure?" He sounded like he was having second thoughts about this plan himself.

"Now, before she gains full control and kills us both!"

He lifted Velsa and tossed her.

CHAPTER FIFTEEN

The moment before Velsa hit the water was the longest of her life. She knew what was coming, and there was nothing she could do.

Shockingly cold water wrapped her in its embrace. She thrashed, even knowing it was futile. Immediately, the water started seeping past her skin, and as it did, the weight of it dragged her under. The current was fast, pulling her along, and she could see nothing. Even if she weren't blindfolded, it was unlikely she would have been able to see in the dark waters.

She kept sinking until her body was scraping rocks on the bottom. She prayed a rock might snag her soon, and then at least she would know she was trapped close to the camp, but the current was unforgiving. She swept along, struggling to gain some purchase. Her stuffing weighed against her bones, but everything was lighter underwater. She wasn't entirely immobile here like she would be on land.

The feeling of it, everything so wet and cold, her head still muddled—panic saturated her as surely as the water did.

Grau! Grau!

She didn't even know if Grau was awake to hear her, and the farther away she was carried, the harder it would be to reach out to him past the restraint of the golden band.

If no one could hear her, she really would be trapped here forever. The waters might carry her so far north that she would

173

freeze. Even if they didn't—

Oh, fates, I can't bear it, this can't be happening!

How long would she have to be here, how terrified and desperate would she have to be, before her soul could ascend? Days, weeks? Grau would be so distraught.

Stop it. He'll search the whole river until he finds you.

She wondered if she could bear such a wait. This might also take days or weeks. Weeks of being so cold, so helpless, voiceless and blind?

Pull yourself together. Surely there is something you can do.

When her feet met rocks, she made an effort to push herself toward the shore. She didn't know which way was home soil and which way was the Miralem lands, but the most important thing was to make herself visible so Grau could find her. The waters fought her, tearing her feet from the ground, but she kept all her focus on this goal.

No, the water was too fast. As soon as she managed a step, it stole her back into its clutches.

With a slam, her body struck a rock. She made a muffled cry of pain, but the worst of the pain faded, leaving only the discomfort of having her arms twisted behind her back. She wouldn't wonder if some of her bones had broken. The current held her there, but for how long?

She was already so exhausted.

Patience, she told herself. *Magic comes from patience. From talking to trees before you need them to talk back. From noticing the smallest things nature has to offer.*

Please...help me. She spoke to the water, although without her crystal it seemed like a dangerous, heedless force. She spoke to the rock, even if it seemed nothing more than a hard lump digging into her arms. *I need to get out of the water. I don't belong here.*

The water rushed by her skin, endless and unfeeling. She was no sorcerer, just a girl who liked to activate a crystal to remind herself she was alive.

Don't panic—no, no, don't panic. Stay focused. She had managed this one moment of composure. She could manage another. She

174

could manage as many as it took. *Your telepathy has more power than the band can contain. You've proved it twice. Get out of the water.*

She concentrated on her body, from head to toe, and imagined herself breaking the surface. She could feel the band's magic straining against her, but she fought—she fought as if she would rather shatter into pieces than let the power go. Her body pushed along the rock and her face broke into dry air. The surface of the rock was above the river waters, and in another moment, her body was sprawled there, back in the element where it belonged. The rock was large enough that only her feet still trailed in the water.

The gag in her mouth felt like a wet sock. She couldn't see a thing. Her limbs were sodden and useless and she'd been stripped down to her chemise and unfastened tunic.

But she was out of the water. She'd done it. A rescue party could see her. She made a choked sound of relief.

Grau…

She fidgeted on the rock, trying to get comfortable where comfort was impossible, especially considering she could barely move. She hoped her stuffing wasn't too out of shape. What a sight she must be.

The cold didn't help either. She had never been *this* cold, so the chill came from the inside. A moment ago, all she wanted was to get out of the water, but now she realized she didn't want to spend any time on this rock either.

She didn't dare move, however, and risk falling back into the water again.

She felt as if she was there for an age, but she must have passed out eventually, because suddenly there was sunlight pouring through her blindfold, and she heard Grau calling her name and splashing through the water.

He ripped off her blindfold. She squinted against the light. By the time he unfastened the gag, she was adjusting to the sunshine and able to look at his face.

He closed up her tunic and took her in his arms. She

realized he was shivering as he splashed back through the water. A few other men had accompanied him, and humiliation swept over her, that anyone should see her so vulnerable.

"What *happened?*" Grau asked.

"Flower. And the guard, Dar."

"I thought as much, but...they dropped you in the water?"

"Obviously."

"Did they—I mean—they didn't do anything else to you, did they?"

"That was all," Velsa said. "But it was enough. Are they back at camp?"

"No. They've vanished."

"Damn it!" Velsa didn't know how she meant to get Flower back for this, but her empathy for the girl had run out entirely. Maybe it was better if she never saw her again, but it was unfinished business.

Yes, if she ever saw Flower again...she would take back her crystal, and that was just for starters.

Velsa couldn't walk; she was regaining motion but she was still too wet. Grau had to carry her home, and as soon as he brought her to bed, she fumbled for the pocket that held the wand. It was still there, thank the stars. Since they were alone, she tapped the band and ripped it off, sighing with relief when the slight warmth of her power returned.

"I'll have to take you to town for repairs," Grau said. "And when I do, I have an idea."

Grau was not able to take her to town right away; his skill at sorcery made him the best tracker in the camp, and Dlara wanted to find the guard who had disappeared with Flower. And Archel, of course, wanted to find Flower herself. As much as Velsa wanted to get back at Flower, she shuddered to think of the girl back in Archel's hands. Truly, he was the monster quietly lurking within the camp.

Grau traced their path down the river, where it disappeared —they must have found or hired a raft or a boat. Maybe Flower

176

had gone to Miralem lands after all, although it was hard to imagine the guard agreeing to that, and he was obviously her lover.

Velsa's limbs had some awkward lumps with her stuffing out of sorts, although her face was all right, so her body could mostly be concealed by her clothes. One of her ribs had broken in two and the loose piece of it kept trying to poke out of her back. She didn't like Grau to look at her although he swore he didn't mind. She had a hard time sleeping, nagged by small discomforts and reliving the memory of the river under her skin.

Finally, after a few days of bad weather, Dlara granted Grau leave to take a day off from the patrol squad, and they rode to town early in the morning. Having her stuffing refreshed was a tedious way to spend time, and she had never been worked on by a stranger. She had only ever been to the Fanarlem repair shop that serviced the House of Perfumed Ribbons. Limb by limb, a young woman split her stitches, pulled out the stuffing pockets around Velsa's bones to replace anything that had gotten too misshapen, and checked the bone itself for cracks, before sewing her skin back up again. Grau read a book while all this went on, except when the woman said, "Sir, did you want to change out the front of her torso today? There's a bit of a stain on her stomach."

"We can live with it."

As it was, Velsa still cringed at the bill for expenses. Archel should have paid for it, if there was any justice, but they had decided that asking him would only make trouble. At least her stuffing was in need of refreshment anyway, and besides the broken rib, her skeleton was intact.

After this, Grau brought her to a magic shop. She hoped he might buy her a new crystal, but instead he went to the counter and said, "Do you have an uncharged golden band?"

"A curious request," the man said.

"I'm a sorcerer myself, so I want to practice charging one."

"Ah! I see. Always nice to see young men interested in the profession. Let me look in back."

Shortly, the man emerged with a band. Since it lacked its most potent magic, it wasn't terribly expensive.

"There we are." Grau handed it to her as they walked out. "A decoy. The men at camp will be none the wiser. I'm sorry I couldn't get you another crystal."

"No—this is better. Much, much better." She pulled him into an alley so she could change the bands that very second. Never again would she wear that accursed thing.

"This is better," he said, taking her hands. "You were right. I should have listened to you, long ago…"

She could feel that his emotions were not quite in line with his words. He seemed a little scared—still. For the first time, he was truly vulnerable against her.

She also sensed that he was fighting it. He didn't want to fear her. Although she couldn't read the specifics of his thoughts, she truly understood that this fear was deep-seated. He had probably been told horror stories of Miralem since he was a boy.

"I understand," she said. "I do. I would never have expected my master to free me of my band, until it was you. I want things so badly. I want to be your wife, and your true partner, so badly that it aches inside me all the time, and I'm impatient."

"You *are* impatient," he said.

"It's turning out that way. In the House, they always said, time and time again, that we were reborn when we were acquired. I always took offense at that; I thought it meant I had to forget my old life and everything that shaped me—well, I think that is what they meant. But it has a new meaning for me. I'm learning who I really am and what I really want."

"I know what you want." He looked at her suggestively.

"Well, not in the *alley*."

He laughed. "I'm talking about pastries. This might be our only trip to town for months, after all. But then, we'll hurry back to camp before the squad returns, see if we can break in that new body of yours."

178

CHAPTER SIXTEEN

Grau held up a jar of honey. "I know where to put it this time."

"I don't know if we should mess with that again."

He raised a brow. "You *need* a little flavor, bellora. Maybe when I have time to develop spells I'll see if I can find a way to make your skin taste delicious."

He took an alarmingly large dollop of honey from the jar and smeared it right on the most sensitive part of her. He pushed her thighs farther apart and his tongue began to tease the center of her desire. At first he was so gentle—too gentle. She tried to be patient, not to beg...to enjoy the tiniest sensations tingling through her reborn body. Maybe this could cleanse away the memory of the cold terror of the river, if she let it all unfold slowly...

His teeth just barely clamped around her clit, slowly closing on her until she let out a little squeal of pain. She pressed her legs around him, and he shoved them apart again.

Now he began to suck the honey away, alternating with digging his tongue into the crevices.

"Oh..." The familiar feeling swept over her, of surrendering to him in the best sort of way, but now that she could feel the ghost of his emotions, now that he finally trusted her without the golden band, her own trust deepened. It was true, that she belonged to him and he belonged, just as much, to her.

She reached for him with her mind—very carefully testing

the waters. Her telepathy was still untrained. She had only used it violently, to protect herself. Never subtly, until now. She would ruin everything if she hurt him.

She didn't try to read him, but simply offered him her own emotions. Her own love, her own lust, the emotional and physical joy rolling through her.

He let out a shuddering sound. "Velsa…what is this?"

"What I'm feeling…"

"*Fates*, I didn't know you could do that. This just got a lot better."

"Not so bad having a…a telepath…" She trailed off into an incoherent little mewl as he returned to his task with renewed vigor. When she shared her sensations with his mind, he knew exactly what to do to render her speechless.

She closed off her mind just before she came, because she knew it would torment him and he'd tormented her often enough.

He looked at her with a wicked smirk. "I ought to spank you for that."

"Go ahead and try. Your mere flesh hand can't do much to me."

He smacked her bottom a few times for good measure anyway; the brief, bright pain only seemed to reinforce the last faint pulses of her climax.

She tossed him a mock glare over her shoulder before turning her attention to his arousal. He had already freed it from his trousers, and she put her mouth around him, teasing the tip with her tongue.

Now it was her turn to feel what he felt; she sensed his willingness to share with her too. She opened her mind, feeling a mirror of every lick and suck in her own hot core. It spurred her on to take him deeper and faster; he was already painfully excited. Her lips and tongue worked quickly as she ran her hands gently up his legs; his muscles were rigid with tension. He lifted her hair up, baring her neck as he reached his release. She groaned as the exquisite pulsing echoed in her own body. She looked at him, dazed, before swallowing his seed.

He gently pushed her down onto the bed and put another dollop of honey in her mouth. She savored its sweetness mingling with the taste of him, closing her eyes, before he kissed her deeply. With the edge of urgency softened from her sharing of thoughts, she opened her mind to him more fully, thinking of Preya's words that she would remove the band so she could give another person all her thoughts. Something in Velsa always yearned to be closer to Grau; she had never imagined she could be so close to anyone. Her childhood had been so lonely, and she bore her loneliness quietly, but she never wanted to feel that way again.

She opened the doors on her yearning, her love, her fears and hopes. Even the fact that sometimes she wanted nothing more than to be his possession, and other times she resented him for the same.

He held her in his arms, he looked at her with his eyes half-closed; mere slits of his brown eyes visible, and she felt his resistance soften. He let her mind reach into his. She had told him that she could already guess his thoughts by now, and indeed, she did not find many surprises. She knew he loved nothing more than to give her a real life and share with her the things he loved—nature and magic and food. She knew he had found her enthralling from the start; that he barely understood it at first and was sometimes ashamed that he had ever gone to the House of Perfumed Ribbons to begin with. She knew he struggled with the way people treated her, that this had taken him off guard.

What did surprise her was the depth of his certainty that she was not a tainted soul. He had *said* he didn't believe it, but she was never sure if attraction had simply overwhelmed belief. From childhood, he would have grown up with Fanarlem servants around, with being told that they were there to serve Daramons. He would have seen the way Fanarlem were depicted in stories and read things like the *Treatise on Fanarlem*, from the Wodrenarune whose word was presented as truth.

181

But just as she had her moment under the moonlight where she knew it wasn't true, his faith in her was just as unshakable.

She started to cry.

"No," he said. "Why cry?"

She shook her head.

"Why is my little marsh toad crying?"

That almost made her laugh.

She felt him raise his resistance to her mind again. "Better to keep a little mystery," he said. "It's almost too much."

She nodded agreement. "I'm glad we shared this once, though. I needed to know how you really feel. It's so hard for me trust." She pressed against him. "Grau, I love you."

It was the first time she had told him. "I love you too, my dearest. But you already know that."

The sound of a piercing siren suddenly tore through the entire camp.

"Damnit, just when I was feeling ready for part two," Grau muttered. "Why do we always get interrupted?" He pulled away from her and looked out the window. "The patrols still aren't back. I hope it's a tornado. The sky is looking pretty nasty in the west."

"You *hope* it's a tornado? I don't know about that! This building is pretty rickety."

He was counting the alarms as he pulled on his clothes. "Five? That can't be all. That's…a severe enemy threat."

"Are we at war? No one's said anything, have they?"

They hurried out to the lawn. Wind scattered papers and leaves. Everyone who remained to defend the camp was gathering. Their numbers were few—twenty or so, and Archel in command. Dlara was out with Grau's usual squad, along with Rawly and everyone they knew best.

If something happened, it couldn't possibly be good to have Archel leading the men. He had made no secret of his resentment that his concubine had run off while Grau and Velsa remained.

The men were pointing, not toward the gray clouds

darkening the western sky, but to a black silhouette that stood against the pale blue sky to the east.

A dragon.

Even from a distance, it could only be a dragon, as large as it was.

Velsa clung to Grau, mesmerized by the sight even as she felt a little weak thinking of the destruction dragons could wreak. She had never expected to see a dragon in her life, and even if it killed her, it was worth taking a moment to appreciate.

"It's real," Grau breathed.

"Well, stop gaping!" Archel cried. "We won't have many chances to get that thing! We need everyone armed with poison on your bullets, and the catapult readied. Sorcerer Thanneau, can you manipulate the wind to get that projectile where it needs to go? Hopefully in its mouth."

"Sir—with all due respect, I don't think we should try to fight the dragon. It'll only anger the beast. Dragons are telepathic. It can deflect my magic easily, and I don't think this would be an easy shot even if it *wasn't* telepathic. We're no match for it. Our best hope is to scatter and hide, and hope it's just passing through."

"Hide? In the woods? Die like cowards?"

"You're saying we should die like an easy target. If we scatter, some of us might live."

"We won't get far enough." Archel's eyes were points of dark fury. "You follow my orders or you leave and I'll report you for insubordination. I won't just sit there and twiddle my fingers while I burn to death."

"This is hopeless," Grau said, as Archel stalked off. "Fighting a dragon is madness, but I suppose it's damned if we do, damned if we don't. If the dragon is coming for us on purpose…our chances are grim no matter what we choose."

"Is there anything I can do?" Velsa asked.

"Just try to keep it from getting in our heads."

She looked around, seeing their small numbers—a handful of men emerging with their rifles, the creaking of the catapult being wheeled around to face the dragon—as if the dragon couldn't change directions the moment it spotted the catapult. They were just going through the motions, weren't they? The camp had never been intended to fight off dragons. It was just a defenseless little outpost.

The dragon was already much closer, no longer just a shadow; she could see the pale color of the scales on its belly.

Lightning split the sky behind them, thunder booming just a moment later. The sky itself seemed to be warning them to hide. Grau turned his face toward the wind. "*That* might be our only hope," he said.

"The storm will scare it off?"

"I've heard that lightning is actually fairly easy to harness…" He turned toward the dragon again, and was quiet, as if it transfixed him. "The last magical beasts in all the world. I almost wish I didn't mind if it killed me."

"Thanneau!" Archel shouted. "Don't just stand there, help us ready more of these poison bullets." He whirled on the camp cook, who was heading for the gate. "And where are you going?"

"Sorry, Lieutenant," the cook said, his face drained of color. "I'm not burning to death."

"Anyone else want to die alone?" Archel barked at the men, sounding panicked. No one else said much, but then, their faces said it all.

It was hard to believe that just moments ago, Velsa had her arms around Grau, warm and content. Now it was possible they might share a horrible end.

She could feel a tingle in her mind, before the dragon was truly upon them. It probed them, probably judging their numbers. She expected its mind to feel much stronger than any person, and somewhat alien besides, but this was not the case. The beast was powerful, yes, but more familiar than she expected. Its thoughts were not so different from hers; this gave her a glimmer of hope.

"Girl."

Velsa realized Archel was speaking to her. She shrunk back.

He had never directly addressed her before. "I have a name," she said.

Grau had moved to help with the bullets, but he was not far away. He and another man were crouched on the ground, picking up bullets with tongs and rolling them in poison dust. Two other men loaded them.

"Velsa," Archel said, and she felt he was suppressing sarcasm. He didn't think much of her, but he *wanted* something. "You're a telepath, aren't you?"

So, word had leaked out. "Yes…"

"You know this might be your chance to protect the life of your beloved Grau."

"I've spoken to her," Grau said. "She will fight with us."

"We could cover *her* in poison. Fling her at the dragon. They find our flesh rather tasty, and if it sees arms and legs flying its way, chances are it will snap her up without realizing."

Grau opened his mouth a few seconds before he found words. "That's—that's insane! You know Lieutenant Dlara would never approve of such a plan. I'm not going to sacrifice Velsa to save the camp. I *will* walk before I let that happen."

"She's a Fanarlem!" Archel snapped. "Our slave. Your slave, yes, but in such a time as this, she is a slave to all people. For the sake of one slave, we might save all the men. It seems such a simple solution. Elegant, really."

Some of the men were watching now, and no one stood up for her besides Grau.

Grau made a move toward Velsa, and Archel seized Velsa's arm. He gestured and some of the other men rushed to his side, surrounding Velsa. A few rifles pointed at Grau.

"This is *no* time to be fighting!" Grau cried. "Look, it's almost here. It can see us by now, I'm sure. Their eyesight is very keen."

"All the more reason why we have to hurry." Archel yanked on Velsa.

She wanted to hurt him. Her powers were blind instinct— no precision, no skill. Just anger and terror, thrust at him from

185

some white hot place deep inside her mind.

The anger wasn't even just for her. It was for Flower, too. She hated Flower, but she hated what Archel had done to her all the more.

Archel screamed like he'd been struck. He clutched his chest and spat blood, then dropped to his knees.

She didn't expect the attack to be so effective, and it made her hesitate. She felt a faint recoil, a brief flash of pain within her own body, and had to pause to master herself—even as a shot cracked in her ears. Someone had fired on Grau, maybe on accident from sheer panic, because no more shots followed. Grau swept an arm at the wind, knocking the arrow from the sky, before Velsa could even think to try and save him herself. If he hadn't been alert for the attack, it would have hit his head.

Everyone was plunged into confusion when Archel collapsed. The catapult wasn't ready. Some of the poisoned rifles were, but everyone looked as if they already knew the dragon would not fall from a few small doses of poison, if they could land a shot at all. None of their plans would come to fruition. The dragon was almost upon them, and they stood paralyzed by its terrible majesty.

To call it an animal or even a beast seemed unfair. It was a beautiful creature, from head to toe, long and slender in body with scales that shone pearlescent on its belly, shading to blue on its back. It seemed like a crystal made flesh. Its wings, too, had a translucent quality, as if they were spun from colored glass. The wings were as wide as the body was long; sweeping waves of air as the dragon came upon them.

It flew low over the camp, scoping them out, before circling round.

Where is the man who bound my friend? The voice that entered Velsa's mind was silken. It might have belonged to a handsome man, with a distinguished accent.

Your telepath? Velsa asked. *Your telepath attacked our camp!*

A Miralem among you? The dragon sounded surprised as it skimmed through the air just above them, as if it wanted to see them closer. Its shadow briefly covered Velsa. *One of the traitors?* *No. A Fanarlem telepath.*

The men fired a volley of shots. The dragon hissed, its body twisting to evade the bullets, its neck whipping round. The wings were spread rigid, catching the wild air of the storm, while it opened its great toothy mouth and released a ball of fire into the headquarters.

This was the least of her worries, but Velsa couldn't help a pang thinking of the burning books, including *Fanarlem Life*, and Grau's bag, which held nothing too special, except the memories of his hands opening the pockets and fishing out various useful items.

Your telepath, she repeated, *attacked* our *camp.* She was probably stupid to argue with a dragon, but the voice in her head seemed so very human, and perhaps even reasonable. *And all we did was put a golden band on her.*

Oh, is that all? As if that is nothing. Those insidious little devices are very difficult to remove without the key. She didn't have the money for removal. I was her only hope for revenge and I hardly need an excuse to attack Daramons. What do you care, little poppet? Aren't you a slave?

Don't tell me you're concerned about my welfare, while you burn up my possessions and threaten my life.

Poor, misguided girl, the dragon said. *They enslaved your people, and they have destroyed mine. I give you two choices: come with me to freedom, or burn with your captors.*

I don't want your forced freedom! Velsa screamed. Her head was throbbing.

The dragon flew high into the sky, and even now she had to watch it, had to admire its shimmering grace. The rain that had been threatening arrived abruptly, the wind lashing against canvas tents. The drops stung her face. She worried about getting wet again—another absurd thought when the dragon might incinerate her.

The dragon swept down, so low that men ran for cover, some of them screaming with unrestrained fear. Its face was going to plow straight into them. Velsa flung herself at Grau. She

187

tried to imagine a layer of protection around them. But she didn't know that she could really protect them. She had the feeble thought that she was glad fire could kill them both. She couldn't bear it if she would live and Grau would die. Weak terror flooded her entire body as she saw the dragon's eyes for the first time, huge golden eyes, as bright as jewels. The dragon's mouth opened —

It snapped up the unconscious Archel and ate him.

Velsa's mouth fell open.

Did you like that? the dragon asked her.

N—no!

Really? I sensed that you didn't care for him.

Velsa really couldn't muster any sympathy for Archel.

The dragon seemed to laugh inwardly. *Is there anyone else here you'd like to me to eat?*

Please! Velsa begged the dragon. *Don't kill anyone else!*

The dragon roared. She almost had the strange feeling that the dragon liked her and wanted her to be impressed that he had killed Archel, and was angry when she didn't offer anyone else to be eaten. She wasn't sure if that was true. It closed her off to its thoughts.

The dragon landed now, flapping its wings so that air and rain flew at them. The men drew back, struggling to keep their rifles aimed. Behind the great wings, smoke billowed from the headquarters, although the rain seemed to be stifling the fire. The dragon's head whipped around and it shot another ball of fire at a row of tents. She could see its face clearly now; narrow horns rising straight from the crown of its graceful head, a few tendrils like whiskers around its nostrils. Rain made the fire smoke and sputter.

I'll ask you again, the dragon said. *Where is the man who banded my telepath?*

He isn't here, Velsa replied. Dlara? Did he really only want Dlara? No, she thought the dragon just enjoyed toying with them.

"Hold him," Grau said.

Hold him?

Did he think she could truly restrain this unearthly creature?

She had to try her best. She reached for the dragon to restrain him.

The dragon immediately sensed her attack. He lifted his head and she expected the fire to come at her any moment. *No— no—no—* She fought to keep the dragon's head pointed at the sky. Her whole body was with her, her toes clenched in her boots, her stuffing feeling tight around her bones all down her arms and legs, her temples searing with agony. It was life or death, seconds ticking by, the dragon's nostrils smoking.

Grau lifted his arms and a bolt of lightning struck the dragon. The dragon screamed, a shrill sound that pierced her ears so sharply that she wouldn't have been surprised if they never worked again.

Grau, too, tried to cover his ears. When the scream ended, the dragon's slender body tumbled to the ground. It fell with a weight she could feel in her feet, and she could hardly bear the sight.

What else could they do, to save their own lives?

A number of the tents in the camp and a few of the latrines were leveled beneath the dragon's body. Its foot crashed into a smoldering campfire, and the flames continue to lap at its claws.

Grau stumbled, clutching her shoulder, but she was ready to collapse herself.

"I'm so sorry," he said. "Fates, I'm sorry. A *dragon.* I've wanted to see one since I was a kid."

"Is it dead?" the men were asking all around them. They fired their rifles again, for good measure.

This seemed too much, to pepper the dragon's shimmering scales with holes when it was obviously dead. *It wasn't a very nice dragon,* she told herself, but knowing that the dragons had lost so much, she couldn't be angry at it. In death, it had a noble expression, but at the same time it was even a little cute.

"This is all your fault, Thanneau." One of the toughest men stalked over to Grau and reached for him.

189

Grau backed away, but he seemed a little dizzy. Velsa went to his side, not that this did any good.

"You and your concubine," the man said. "I heard that your concubine got in the fight with the Miralem in the first place, and you wouldn't listen to Archel, and you killed the damn dragon."

"*And?*" Grau demanded. "I fail to see how killing the dragon, which was Archel's entire plan, was an error on my part. And the Miralem attack before had nothing to do with Velsa."

"It just isn't right, a telepathic Fanarlem. These things are attracted to her."

"Telepathic?" a skinny man asked.

"That's what I heard!" the first man said. "She probably told the dragon to kill Archel!"

More voices of protest joined in.

"We need to concentrate on putting out the fires!" Grau said. "I really don't think you want to attack us."

"You seem pretty exhausted."

"We could say the dragon ate you, too..."

"The world might be better off without a skarnwen and his slave..."

"Grau!" Velsa shrieked as one of the men fired behind Grau, and this time, he didn't have time to deflect. The bullet struck his shoulder.

"Back off or I'll kill you all," Velsa said, as some of them edged closer.

"Yes, back off!" Grau said. "I just killed a dragon, damn it!"

"Grau—we need to leave," she said, but she could tell from the mood in camp that they couldn't go without a fight.

"I need to put out the fire!" he said. "Or our squad will come back and find they have no shelter..." He let out a small gasp of pain, but he started running. *Outrunning the poison,* she thought.

A few of the soldiers followed, to keep an eye on them, but mostly they seemed to realize the sense of letting Grau staunch the flames at headquarters. The rain had kept it from going up completely, and maybe it had fireproofing spells placed upon it as important buildings often did, but smoke was trailing from one corner of the roof.

Grau made it to the building, but then he stopped and leaned against a post, his face drenched in rain and sweat. His color was positively sickly. "Can you get the bullet out?" he asked her. "My body can heal, but only if you get it out."

"I think so…" She placed her hand on his shoulder, extending her telepathy to feel through his damaged flesh. She hated this, dealing with flesh and blood when it got messy and painful, but she closed her eyes and tried to pull the bullet out again.

He barked out a barely restrained sound of pain as the bullet fell to the ground.

"Oh, no, I'm sorry, I don't think I did a very good job."

"How were you able to stop *Fern's* pain and not mine?"

"I don't know how I did it! Where is your healing potion?"

"In my bag. In our room…" He dropped to his knees.

She looked back and what did she see, but a man applying healing potion to some petty little arm wound not five feet away. As soon as she saw him, he put it away and turned his back on her.

She ran after him. "You *fiend*, you won't help Grau when he's trying to save headquarters? Look, he's passing out!"

"What do headquarters benefit me?" he said sullenly. "I sleep in a tent, not a fancy officer's bed. I can't read those books. I don't really care if Dlara has a desk. You know benefited me? Flower."

He grabbed her hand and lifted her off the ground, dangling by one arm. "I'm not afraid of you. They say you're telepathic? Well, show me something."

She reached for his pocket and tried to use telekinesis to pluck out the healing potion, but her head was still throbbing from fighting the dragon. She couldn't quite seem to catch it and quickly, her panic rose. "Put me down!" Her mind was going back to having her hands tied behind her back, the complete helplessness of being unable to fight Flower and the guard.

Grau lurched forward to help her. "Let her *go*."

"Or what?" The man shook Velsa by the arm.

This seemed to break her paralysis, so she could rake at him with her mental weapons. "There she goes," he said, encouraging the other men to rush to his aid. One man kicked Grau in the stomach and Velsa screamed, wincing. She felt how much these men hated her and Grau—why? Some of them believed they were an affront to fate itself, and others were jealous of Grau for having enough money to buy a concubine. Potent fear mingled with their anger. Many of them had believed the dragon would kill them. They didn't understand why the dragon would come, if not because it was drawn by the only other magical being among them—Velsa.

Velsa could feel something inside her like the very storm itself, that could destroy and leave her wondering what on earth she had done. This was the power Grau was afraid of. Her head was splitting open.

Outside the gates came the sound of horses and shouted voices.

Fates! The patrol!

The gate was unattended, and Dlara rushed through at the front, his rifle at the ready. The man put Velsa down, but not before Dlara saw him. Dlara barely noted the dragon corpse before leading his mount around the camp debris.

"What is going on here?" he shouted. "What happened? Where is Lieutenant Archel?"

"Dead," a few people said at once.

"Then, Sorcerer Thanneau, you are the highest ranking person who was here for the dragon attack. Tell me what happened."

"The dragon appeared..."

"Are you hurt?" Dlara dismounted.

"Yes," Grau said, curtly. "I was shot and kicked in the stomach by—him, and him." He pointed.

"All right, *look*." Dlara turned on the surly expression of the men gathered around. "I have tolerated far more of this than I should, because Archel fought my efforts to maintain order at every turn, but I will not tolerate you attacking the only sorcerer in our camp."

"He'd be all right on his own." The man who had lifted Velsa by her arm spoke. "It's his concubine. She's *telepathic*."

Dlara stalked over to the man. "I saw you grabbing her," he said. "I am aware she is telepathic. It is not your place to decide whether her presence is safe. She saved our damned *lives*." He struck the man across the face.

She tried not to think of what she might have done, if they had come five minutes later. And if she wasn't able to fight, what the men might have done to her and Grau...

What they might do, the moment Dlara turned his back.

"We have buildings on fire, we have a dragon corpse, we have a lieutenant dead," Dlara said. "This is no time to be worrying over a concubine. Garman, get your men working on putting out the fires. Drinna, ride to town and tell them we need help with removing the dragon. The rest of you, take care of the wounded and support Garman."

Rawly threw his arms around Grau.

"Please, Rawly...it's my turn to be dying," Grau said.

"Ah...I see that now. I thought you were just wet. But you haven't pissed yourself. We ran into the cook on the way in, and...well. I can't blame him."

Grau sighed. "I'm not sure we're welcome here any more, Rawly."

"Aw," Rawly said, like he couldn't quite believe it.

No, they weren't really safe even now. Besides their own squad, the men were still glaring, muttering, pointing. Even in Grau's squad, she couldn't trust the mood not to turn once the story was told and twisted. And they would all know, now, that either her golden band was a decoy, or her powers were much stronger than the band.

Dlara came to see them after delegating some orders. By

193

this time, Grau and Velsa had taken shelter in the stable so Velsa stayed dry, although the rain was slowing now. They had already saddled Fern. Rawly had fetched Grau some healing potion, and he was looking much better.

"Sir—" Grau started to stand, but Dlara waved him back down onto the stool where he had been resting.

Dlara crossed his arms. "This is quite a mess. This camp is unlikely to be quiet ever again, now that we've killed a dragon. I'd be sorry to lose you two...but the suspicion of Velsa has become too dangerous. I'm willing to discharge you officially, but I don't know where you can go..." He glanced outside and then noticed the stablehand. "Barlem, would you mind stepping out a moment?"

"No, sir."

"Have you ever considered...claiming her as a flesh-born Fanarlem?"

Velsa gripped her hands together.

"I have," Grau said carefully.

"I think it would be wise."

"You really think so?"

"The thing is, whether or not it's true that Fanarlem are meant to be slaves, she has done her duty. She's protected us and she obviously makes you happy. This cruelty is unwarranted, and so I would be willing to notarize a birth record for her. But I'll also have to claim that you brought her into this camp illegally, claiming she was a concubine so you could have your wife with you, and that I docked your pay accordingly. Which *will* make you seem a bit eccentric. But you'll need a story to take home with you."

"Sir—I hardly know what to say. Sounds like you've thought about this as much as I have."

"I doubt it." Dlara smirked.

"I can't go home, though," Grau said. "My father knows Velsa is no flesh-born Fanarlem and he would never play along. I need to put as much distance between this place and home as I can."

"That's a shame," Dlara said.

"I've been considering going to Nalim Ima. You've been there, haven't you?"

"Yes," Dlara said. "It's a very advanced nation. Surprises at every turn. I think you'd both enjoy it."

"Do you think they'd treat Velsa well?"

"If they think she's flesh-born, I'm sure they will. And I can tell you, I expect you'll see plenty of phonographs."

That very night, Dlara made up all the requisite papers. "I've broken more than a few laws tonight," he said. "But I'm betting all the distraction of dragons at the border will keep anyone from noticing. Still, be smart. Keep your secrets for all of our sake."

They exchanged bows with Dlara—and offered him profuse thanks. Velsa hardly knew what to say.

"Don't look so happy," Dlara said. "I'm afraid the world might get a lot uglier before long. Enjoy your happiness, may it last you for decades to come."

They said goodbye to Rawly, who hardly seemed to notice the weight of what had happened, and merely invited them to stay with him in his hometown any time.

They set off for the town. The rain had stopped, and town was close enough that they could still get a decent sleep. They had just been there that morning for her repairs, after all, but that seemed like a week ago already.

Velsa stared at the humble, hand-written paper Dlara had made up, with a eighteen-years-past date and a fictional signature, asserting that she had been born Velsa Biarnan, to a Halnari Miralem mother and a Daramon father, in the city of Nisa.

The rest of her false story, she would have to imagine for herself.

"So, I suppose this means we're married," Grau said. "I hope you didn't want a big wedding."

She scoffed. "I don't need a wedding," she said, "as long I get a wedding night."

Also in the Hidden Lands Series

THE ATLANTIS FAMILIES
(Young Adult Fantasy)
Book One: The Vengeful Half
Book Two: The Stolen Heart
Book Three: TBA

THE TELEPATH AND THE SORCERER
(Fantasy Romance)
Book One: The Sorcerer's Concubine
Book Two: The Sorcerer's Wife, Fall 2016
Book Three: The Sorcerer's Equal, TBA

Also By Jaclyn Dolamore

From Bloomsbury:

Magic Under Glass

Magic Under Stone

Between the Sea and Sky

From Hyperion:

Dark Metropolis

Glittering Shadows

About the Author

Jaclyn Dolamore has a passion for history, vintage dresses, David Bowie, anime, and food. She lives with her partner and plot strategist Dade and three weird cats in an 140-year-old house in western Maryland. She loves to hear from readers!

Twitter: @jackiedolamore

Blog: jaclyndolamore.blogspot.com

DeviantArt: jaclyndolamore.deviantart.com

45517010R00114

Made in the USA
Lexington, KY
17 July 2019